SINKING DEEPER

~~UK~~

~~awesome~~ ~~brilliant~~ Heroic

My ~~Questionable~~ Decision to Invent a Sea Monster

Steve Vernon

NIMBUS
PUBLISHING

Nimbus Publishing Limited
PO Box 9166, Halifax, NS B3K 5M8
(902) 455-4286 www.nimbus.ca

Printed and bound in Canada
Nimbus Publishing is committed to protecting our
natural environment. As part of our efforts, this book
is printed on 100% recycled content paper.

Design: Jennifer Embree
Author photo: Belinda Ferguson

This novel is a work of fiction. Names, characters, places, and incidents are either the product of the author's imagination or are used fictitiously. Any resemblance to actual persons, living or dead, events or locales is entirely coincidental.

Library and Archives Canada Cataloguing in Publication

Vernon, Steve
Sinking deeper, or, My questionable
(possibly heroic) decision to invent
a sea monster / Steve Vernon.
ISBN 978-1-55109-777-0

I. Title.
PS8593.E774S56 2011   jC813'.6   C2010-908141-2

The Canada Council | Le Conseil des Arts
for the Arts | du Canada

Tourism, Culture and Heritage

We acknowledge the financial support of the Government of Canada through the Book Publishing Industry Development Program (BPIDP) and the Canada Council, and of the Province of Nova Scotia through the Department of Tourism, Culture and Heritage for our publishing activities.

Dedicated to my grandfather Hanlan Arthur Vernon,
who told me more stories than he ever knew.

PART I

THE CABER CAPER

Chapter 1

ALARM CLOCKS COME IN ALL SHAPES AND SIZES

My first jailbreak began when a coarse-toothed mechanic's file crashed through the window of the Deeper Harbour Police Station at two in the morning. The file bounced three or four times before clattering to a halt among a scatter of shattered glass. The file spun a little and came to rest, like a compass needle pointing somewhere far off the edge of the map. Looking back from right here and right now I believe I would like to start this story right then—three days after I had just turned fourteen—spending my birthday in jail.

My name is Roland Diefenbaker McTavish. I don't know what Dad was thinking when he gave me the middle name Diefenbaker, but I bet you he was giggling when he did it. That's how it goes when you're a kid. You really don't have much say in what happens to you, and your parents usually laugh at you if you think you do.

As for the file flying through the window—well, I guess it was time to wake up.

"Hsssst," a voice whispered from outside the broken window.

I shook the pillow feathers out of my ear-holes and squoodged the sleep-sand out of my eyeballs with the sides of my fists.

"Hsssst."

What was that noise?

"Hsssst."

Either my ears had sprung a long, slow leak or I was about to be broken out of jail by the world's largest boa constrictor.

"Hsssst."

"If you're trying to whistle, take the soda crackers out of your mouth," I suggested, "because all of this hssssting is beginning to royally hsssst me off."

"Roland, it's me," Dulsie whispered.

I knew it was her. Who else was going to wake me up from a sound sleep to break me out of my jail cell if it wasn't Dulsie Jane Boudreau?

"Are you awake?" Dulsie asked.

"I am now."

I swung my feet off of my cot and the rest of me followed. I was wearing a pair of jeans that stank and stood up with me as if I'd been wearing them for three days straight—which I had.

Dad wasn't all that big on doing laundry.

"Hurry up," Dulsie said. "I don't want your dad to catch us."

"Dad's on patrol," I said, which meant he'd gone down the street and opened the back door to Nora's Diner to make himself a deep-fried grilled cheese sandwich, his favourite midnight snack. Dad had eaten a lot of sandwiches in the two years since he and Mom had decided that getting almost-divorced was the best way to stay sort-of friendly. "He won't be back for a while."

There wasn't exactly what you'd call a criminal element here in Deeper Harbour. In fact, the last big crime wave had involved a dropped potato chip bag, an unlicensed Labrador retriever, and somebody spitting bubblegum onto the sidewalk.

"Did you have to break the window?" I asked.

"It wasn't my idea," Dulsie said. "Blame your granddad."

Dulsie didn't need to be afraid of what Dad would do about the broken window. That was strictly my problem. Even if I had a video of Dulsie flinging that file through the window, along with her fingerprints and enough DNA to spell the word "and" about ten thousand times or so, I'd still wind up being blamed.

That's just how things roll here in Deeper Harbour.

"I broke the window," Granddad Angus confessed from the shadows. "Now stand back. I'm going to kick down this door."

That figured. Aside from Dulsie, my granddad was the most likely person to be staging my first ever jailbreak. The two of them were my very best friends and they drove me crazy as only best friends can.

"Don't break the door," I said. "I'll be in enough trouble for the window."

I pulled on my t-shirt, which was a little cleaner than my jeans— but not much. I stepped into my running shoes and worked my feet down through the double knots before making my getaway—meaning, I opened the cell door, which Dad never locked. The jail cell was where I slept on nights when I wasn't at home with Mom. Dad's idea of divorce gave a whole new meaning to the word "custody."

As far as I could remember I was the only person who'd spent a night in the cell in years, which should tell you something about Deeper Harbour.

"Did you really have to break the window?" I asked Granddad Angus. "You could have just tapped on the door and I'd have opened it. I'm sure Dad keeps a key under the doormat."

"Breaking the window was much more dramatic," Granddad Angus explained. "You can't live the story of your life properly without the occasional addition of a little sudden drama."

Granddad Angus had a theory. He believed that life was nothing more than a story we told ourselves. A story that would not reveal its ending until we finally got there and found out just what we had been trying to tell ourselves all along.

"Hurry up," Granddad Angus said. "The last thing I need is to be yelled at by Police Chief McTavish."

Let me see if I can hack down the family tree so that you can have a better look at each knothole and twig.

Police Chief McTavish is my dad. That makes me his son, which is what he usually calls me. Granddad Angus is my dad's dad, and I'm the one at the end—mostly stuck in the middle.

Have you got that straight?

I opened the outside door. The first thing I saw was Granddad Angus, wearing his kilt and his backwards fanny pack, a faded blue t-shirt that read, "Bagpipes Blow, Big Time," a pair of floppy, red plaid running shoes, and his magic fishing vest of many pockets. All of that and a grin so big and so wide he looked as if he was getting set to tell the entire known universe the single greatest knock-knock joke in history.

I should tell you a little about Granddad Angus's magic fishing vest of many pockets. I don't think the vest is actually magical, but it sure seemed that way. It was battered and old with pockets sewn onto pockets and a few more pockets hidden under pockets that you couldn't see. The vest was a sort of warm, soft toolbox with armholes, and Granddad Angus had worn it since I could remember. Truthfully, I think Granddad Angus was born wearing it.

As far as I could tell, Granddad Angus's magic fishing vest of many pockets had nearly everything in it you could dream of and a lot more that you couldn't. I had seen Granddad Angus pull a jackknife, a twist of twine, a stick of chewing gum, postage stamps, silver dollars, a pocket watch, and a screwdriver out of it. Dad told me that one Christmas Granddad Angus pulled an entire electric train set out of those vest pockets—one car and one piece of track at a time—and I believed it.

Dulsie was different. *Different* was the best word I could ever use to describe her. She was wearing black jeans with Hello Kitty patches sewn on each of the legs, a baseball hat with a picture of Happy Bunny on it, and a black t-shirt that read "CATS" underneath a pair of bright yellow cat eyes. She'd painted a mask on her face with greasepaint and streaked a set of whiskers on both sides of her nose.

"So what are you supposed to be today?" I asked, because I knew she wanted to be asked.

Dulsie wanted a real tattoo real bad, only she couldn't afford one. Also, there wasn't a tattoo shop in town. Also, her dad wouldn't let her get a for-real tattoo over his for-real dead body—and so far he looked pretty healthy to me.

So Dulsie invented the today tattoo.

Every morning she painted a new design on her face or her arms or anywhere else she decided. Every night she washed it off in the shower and most likely lay awake half the night dreaming up her next today tattoo just in time for tomorrow.

"I'm a cat burglar. Get it?" she said.

I got it, and I thought she looked a little goofy and way too kiddish in her cat burglar makeup and too-big t-shirt, but I told her she looked pretty cool—which is a word that nobody but my dad ever says anymore. I caught that word from Dad like you might catch a case of the measles.

I lied to Dulsie about being cool because she was my best friend. Dulsie hugged me thanks. Being fourteen, I usually hated being hugged by girls, but lately Dulsie's hugs hadn't felt quite as bad. I knew that her whiskers and mask were probably smearing off on my shirt, but like I said, my shirt was dirty to begin with.

"We're breaking you out of jail whether you like it or not," Dulsie told me.

Dulsie was Deeper Harbour's first and only punk-goth-freakazoid. At least, that's what she called herself. I didn't know exactly what a punk-goth-freakazoid was, but whatever it was, Dulsie was definitely one of them. She dressed in denim and leather and bike chains, her hair usually looked as if she had washed it in a box of crayons, and every morning brought a new today tattoo.

I wouldn't tell her this, but I think Dulsie liked her paint more than she would a for-real tattoo. You see, you can change paint and you can't change a tattoo, and change was absolutely unpredictable—just like Dulsie.

"I don't see why you're going to all this trouble anyway," I said.

"You've been moping," Granddad Angus said.

"I have not."

Dulsie nodded, agreeing with Granddad Angus. Didn't I hate it when my two best friends ganged up on me like this—which they usually did.

"You have been moping. I recognize a case of mid-summer mope. It's utterly unmistakable and the best cure for a mope is to get up and do something," Dulsie said. "So come on, let's get busy and get doing. Your granddad has a plan."

There was no point in arguing. The window was broken and so was my sleep. Besides, they were right. I had been moping. I stepped over the broken window glass, which crunched like a carpet of Kellogg's Corn Flakes. I told myself not to worry about the window.

What was the worst thing Dad could do?

Lock me in jail?

"Better grab that file," Dulsie said. "I wouldn't want your dad CSI-ing that for evidence."

Now I didn't think Dad could spell CSI if you wrote it out for him in big, loud, capital letters, but I was too tired to argue. I hadn't looked at the alarm clock, but I knew by now it said two-thirty in the morning.

Time is funny like that.

It'll run out and run over and run away on you whether you're looking at it or not.

Towns are built that way, too.

Sometimes, so are people.

Chapter 2

SMASHING PUMPKINS

Chud-chudda-chuck-chudda.

Fifteen minutes later, the three of us stood in Molly Winter's prize-winning pumpkin patch using a gigantic two-handed antique bucksaw to cut down the pole that was holding up Molly's laundry line. Actually, antique wasn't an old enough word. The saw looked nearly freaking prehistoric.

"This'll fix her for sure," Dulsie said. "That petrified old she-bat."

Molly was our school librarian. She was a large, frumpy woman who wore dresses that might once have been tents. As far as I could tell, Molly had been gifted with the magic ability to find whatever book you were looking for, even if you didn't know what you were looking for.

Chud-chudda-chuck-chudda.

I didn't have any particular grudge against Molly or her clothesline pole, but Dulsie sure did. You see, Molly had told Dulsie she couldn't come into the library painted the way she was, which at the time was a chessboard pattern, complete with a pair of plastic pawns she had tied to her ears with string. Getting her ears pierced was another one of those over-my-dead-body rules of her dad's.

"Well, how would you like to see me painted?" Dulsie had asked Molly, which went over like a baked-bean bugle-fart.

Chud-chudda-chuck-chudda.

The saw blade chudded, chucked, chattered, and bounced at first, skipping over the wood grain instead of cutting straight through it, until the teeth finally sank into the deeper timber and the cut began to properly take.

"Come on to her, boy," Granddad Angus prompted. "Muckle onto this saw good and proper."

There were days when Granddad Angus needed subtitles.

There were days when all the subtitles in China couldn't help.

Granddad Angus almost never said anything that didn't mean something else. The man talked in code. When he said, "come on to her," he really meant "bear down hard," which was just another way of saying "muckle onto this," which was another way of saying "get cracking and come a daisy onto her."

Have you got that straight?

Me neither.

"Are you sure this saw is sharp enough?" I asked.

"Sure as glue," Granddad Angus said. "I spent the last week setting the teeth on this old misery whip to the perfect angle. This saw will cut a thin fog from the broad edge of a cloudy morning."

"You're not cutting fog," Dulsie pointed out. "You're cutting down a clothesline pole."

I took the opportunity to point out that some people—namely, my dad—might look at what we were doing as an act of criminal vandalism.

"You're both wrong. What we're doing is having an adventure," Granddad Angus replied. "And adventure is a long-winded way of saying fun."

"So are we having fun yet?" I asked.

"Fun is what you make of it. We're not cutting down a clothesline pole. We are freeing up a caber that has been disguised all these years as a laundry accessory."

A caber is a tree trunk, as big and as tall as a telephone pole, that is meant to be run with and thrown end over end as a test of strength. If you ever figure out why someone would want to throw a telephone pole, let me know. I just don't get it.

"If you say so," I replied, still not convinced.

"We are what we are until we become something else," Granddad Angus explained patiently. "That is the magic of evolution, time, and change. This pole used to be a Jack pine until someone cut it down. We're just freeing a caber that's spent a lifetime trapped inside a clothesline pole that used to be a Jack pine."

I was sure what Granddad Angus was saying made perfect sense in some alternate universe, but I still didn't get it—and I didn't really need to. He was my Granddad Angus and my very best friend and I would do just what he asked me to.

"Let's get to the timbering," he said. "Lean on your end of the saw and I'll haul on mine. Dulsie, you keep watch. If this pole falls on us and kills us both dead, it'll be your job to bury our remains under one of these pumpkins."

So I leaned and he hauled and I let him pull me along. I stopped arguing and got into the spirit of the thing and before too long that old saw stopped chucking and chudding and settled into a groove.

I'm not saying the cutting was smooth or consistent, you understand. The fact was, that old saw sounded like an asthmatic bulldog working out a case of terminal lockjaw on an arthritic mailman's ankle bone. I couldn't believe Molly Winter could sleep through a racket that was ten times worse than bagpipes, scalded cats, and a snowplow scraping down a frozen gravel road.

All at once the pole gave way to gravity and came crashing straight down. Granddad Angus dropped the saw and caught the pole with both of his palms, and ran backwards, hand-over-handing the caber down to the dirt—at least until he tripped over me.

I hadn't planned on tripping Granddad Angus. I was too busy trying to duck down and get out of the way of that two-hundred-pound, timber-tumbling, clothesline-pole people-squasher to make any kind of plan. Fortunately, the pole missed both of us and broke its fall on Molly Winter's prize-winning pumpkin patch, which, given the mess we'd made, probably wasn't winning too many prizes this year.

"What a mess," I said, staring at a dozen or so freshly flattened jack-o-pancakes.

"Those pumpkins look more like squash, right now," Granddad Angus replied, thoughtfully stroking the salt and pepper of his beard.

"I'm going to get blamed for this, too," I predicted.

"Me too," Dulsie said, looking over her shoulder towards Molly's darkened house. "I hope my dad doesn't get too mad at me."

"There's no need to blame anyone," Granddad Angus said. "Squint properly and you'll see this is nothing more than a freshly planted field of Nova Scotia Jack pine pumpkins. Come next year, a newborn Jack pine will shoot up from that spot, sprouting limbs full of fat orange pumpkins so big and so round and so orange that the coyotes will howl every night thinking that they're staring up at a tree full of full moon."

Have I mentioned Granddad Angus's wild-as-the-wind imagination?

"That is about the single stupidest thing you've ever said," I pointed out, not wanting to encourage such flights of fancy.

"You sound like your father," Granddad Angus said. "You don't really mean it."

Don't really mean it?

I guess I didn't really mean it when I told Granddad Angus that sticking postage stamps to a fresh mackerel, addressing it to the Department of Fisheries, and dropping it into a mailbox to complain about their latest policy was not all that clever a plan.

I guess I didn't really mean it when I told Granddad Angus that painting sunflowers on roadkill didn't qualify as beautifying the town.

And I guess I didn't really mean it when I told Granddad Angus it was a bad idea to put wagon wheels on a dory, hop inside, and roll the dory-wagon straight down Dead Dog Hill with only a hockey helmet and three pillows duct-taped to his behind for protection.

"What sort of a story is your life going to be if you don't learn to turn up your imagination every chance you get?" Granddad Angus asked. "That's the problem with you movie-watching, video-game-playing, cell-phoning kids these days. You haven't learned to turn on the lights in your imagination yet."

And that's right about when Molly's bedroom light turned on.

Chapter 3

KAMIKAZE CABER CHUCK

Granddad Angus once told me the story of the Cape Breton Blue Mountain Banshee, a fiendish she-devil who would wail and scream and raise a racket just before somebody dropped stone-cold dead. Well, let me tell you, Molly wailed and screamed loud enough to make a full-grown banshee drop dead.

Dulsie did the smartest thing I'd ever seen a punk-goth-freakazoid do; namely, she took off running in the other direction. The last thing I saw was her chartreuse hair cat-burglaring right through the open garden gate. I admired her running form and wished I could run that fast or even in that direction, but there was no way on earth I could bail on Granddad Angus.

"Grab the caber," Granddad Angus shouted.

He snatched up one end and I grabbed the other and we both started running. After cutting down Molly's clothesline pole and flattening her pumpkins, there wasn't anything left undestroyed except the garden fence. That is, until we knocked it over as we performed a battering-ram escape manoeuvre, which felt a little like I was leading a fast avalanche down the side of a cliff.

I kept on running and didn't stop until Granddad Angus told

me to. We were halfway down the middle of Deeper Harbour's main street, meaning the only paved street in town.

"Straighten the caber out," Granddad Angus ordered breathlessly.

I was still trying to catch up to my own breath, but I stooped and picked my end of the caber back up and we laid it down the centre line of the road—or at least where we remembered the line to have been. It hadn't been repainted since a little more than two years ago, back when they paved the new highway that went around Deeper Harbour, cutting it off from the rest of the world.

At that point, Deeper Harbour basically fell off the map. In fact, the whole town might as well have fallen into the harbour. We could still get to the highway, but we had to go through two other towns to do it.

"Are we ready?" I asked.

"Almost," Granddad Angus said, taking his hat off. "A few words need to be said."

"Say them fast," I recommended.

I could still hear Molly wailing away.

Granddad Angus wasn't hurrying. He reached into his fanny pack. He called that fanny pack his sporran, but I knew a backwards fanny pack when I saw one. He fished out a can of Coke. He opened it up and handed the can to me. He reached into a pocket of his many-pocketed vest and drew out two shiny silver shot glasses.

"Pour them both," he ordered. "There needs to be a speech."

Granddad Angus loved his speeches.

"Molly Winter's clothesline pole grew up from a Jack pine that stood watch over Deeper Harbour ever since Samuel Champlain

sailed past back in the early seventeenth century and rudely refused to stop."

I set the can down on the pavement. Meanwhile, Molly kept
wailing. By now her wailing sounded almost musical, as if she'd
figured out how to harmonize panic.

"The Jack pine stood there until some Acadian lumberjack
lopped the tree down to hang Molly Winter's sopping wet sail-wide
granny panties on—so I don't believe it will mind being trans-
formed from a clothesline pole to a caber."

"Amen," I said, hoping to hurry him along.

"Bottoms up," he added, tipping his glass straight back.

I tossed the Coke in my mouth and took a hard swallow.

"Good?" Granddad Angus asked.

"Good." ·

"Should we chuck the caber uphill or down?" he asked.

"Uphill," I decided.

"Why's that?"

"Because I want to see if you can throw it hard enough and far
enough to clear a path to the new highway."

Granddad Angus grinned, spit on his hands, and pointed uphill. The two of us hand-over-handed the clothesline-pole caber
upright. Then he crouched down, taking the proper caber-chuck-
ing stance while I did my best to keep it propped up.

The knots in Granddad Angus's knees creaked and popped. He
grunted as he laced his hands about the girth of the pole and slowly
stood up. Just for an instant he stood there, the caber pointing towards the heavens in true Celtic caber-tossing style.

And then the caber began to tip slowly backwards.

Granddad Angus backpedalled with the big pole, finding his

footing and twisting his direction as he went. I stepped backwards with him, kicking over the can of Coke. The spilled pop made a wet hissing sound as it fizzled into the dirt—like the sound of a burning dynamite fuse.

Then Granddad Angus starting running with the caber. He headed downhill towards the wharf, our plan of chucking uphill discarded in the name of gravity, momentum, and plain common sense.

I ran alongside Granddad Angus, wishing I could keep some distance between me and that clothesline-pole kid-crusher, but he was my granddad and I would not let him run on alone.

We kept on running as the road galloped towards the wharf.

The ocean beyond got closer.

The caber started to tip.

"Chuck it, Granddad," I shouted. "Chuck it!"

He tried his best to keep up with the momentum of the twenty-foot clothesline-pole caber running madly away with itself. I saw Dulsie's dad Warren's boat shed flash past like a falling-down, paint-peeling, two-by-four comet. We hit the bottom of the hill and straightened out just long enough for Granddad Angus to un-successfully attempt to hide his panic.

"Chuck it," I gasped, but the words came out something like, "Muck-phht."

Granddad Angus grunted and gripped the caber as best he could. Just for an instant, I imagined that the soul of that Nova Scotia Jack pine had shot its laundry-stained essence down through the tangle of arthritic knots in Granddad Angus's hands, angling through his knees and ankles and funky old kilt, straight on down into the dirt of that Maritime shoreline.

And then Granddad Angus let the caber fly free.

Picture the world's ugliest totem pole taking flight. Throw in a little bit of rocket-to-the-moon, three measures of I-think-I-can-I-think-I-can, and a twist of crossed fingers for dumb luck, and you're somewhere close to the notion of pure, unleashed caber-hood.

The caber shot straight up and toppled end-over-end upon the pavement in front of the shaky old wharf, continuing right on over the edge, and then—heavy end first—it smacked straight into the belly of Warren Boudreau's dory, torpedo-holing the little wooden craft straight through.

For about three-quarters of a minute the sight of that capsized and caber-impaled dory was a truly grand and wonderful sight.

"Now what?" I asked. "Should we run?"

Granddad Angus couldn't answer. He was too busy leaning against a weathered grey wharf piling, his hands spider-splayed about the curved timber, trying unsuccessfully to catch his breath.

It was times like these that I realized I had almost forgotten how old my grandfather really was. He usually seemed like a grey-haired schoolkid out for recess and ready to play. Now, looking at him, I saw the old man who was hiding behind his knock-knock-joke grin—pale and sweating, his eyes holding nothing but a deep, faraway stare...interrupted by my dad, walking slowly towards us, still wiping deep-fried grilled cheese sandwich crumbs from the dirty red thicket of his beard. Granddad Angus's saw was tucked under Dad's arm, so I guess he'd already visited Molly's shamelessly demolished pumpkin patch.

"You dropped your saw," Dad said.

He sounded almost helpful.

Granddad Angus managed a weak hello grin.

"Only a mule-headed Scotsman would think it a sport to steal a clothesline pole and run the length of a football field to heave it," Dad observed as he stood there scratching his head and leaning on the wharf's teetering railing, staring out at the wreckage of a caber-stuck dory.

Bedroom lights all around the harbour snapped on and people poked their noses out their bedroom windows. Deeper Harbour is awfully quiet most of the time, so a commotion like this was bound to wake up the whole town.

"Well," Granddad Angus said, "at least we gave them something to look at."

I stood beside my dad, staring at Warren Boudreau's impaled dory drifting sadly across the lonely goodbye gulp of Deeper Harbour. The caber stuck straight up out of the smashed gut of the pine-and-oak dory, looking a little like some weird, petrified, prehistoric sea creature, drifting in the lee and gentle swallow of the harbour.

It was most definitely something to look at. And looking back at that long-ago-then from the safety of my right-about-now, I think that was the exact moment I first started to kick around my crazy idea to revive a dead town.

Chapter 4

THE YOWLING HOWL OF A MUSICAL SAW

BANG—clack.

The second scariest sound I ever heard was the slam of the cell door and the clack of the bolt latching shut as Dad locked Granddad Angus and me in jail—for real.

"You need to consider the consequences of your actions," Dad told me while he patched the broken window with a flattened cardboard box.

"Consequences" is one of those words—like "responsibility," "expectations," and "homework"—that grown-ups feed you. One of those words that tastes like spoonfuls of boiled, unbuttered, un-salted, and un-cheese-sauced cauliflower. I tasted that word while Granddad Angus rattled the steel window-breaking file against the cell bars—clanter, clanter, clanter.

Dad banged the last tack into the cardboard window patch, which fell to the glass-strewn floor at the exact moment that some-one banged hard on the outside door.

THUDTHUDTHUDTHUD.

"Maybe it's the prime minister of Canada," Granddad Angus guessed. "Come to Deeper Harbour to hand out dory-sinking medals."

"There is no way on earth the prime minister would come to a hole in the coast like Deeper Harbour," I said. "I don't even know what we're doing here."

Do you think I was being too hard on our town?

Let me put it in perspective for you.

If you look at a globe you'll see Canada, a big stretch of open country that sits on top of the United States like a huge maple-leaf-scented, beaver-skin hat. At the eastern corner of Canada is the province of Nova Scotia, stretched out like a beached giant squid, with the Yarmouth, Digby, and Bridgewater end being its head and its tentacles wiggling up around the high country in Cape Breton Island.

Now get out your biggest magnifying glass and have a peek at the stretch south of Yarmouth and north of Cape Sable. Keep on squinting. Do you see that little fly pimple of a harbour just next to the town of Goodbye and Good Riddance and I Hope You Don't Drown on the Way Out With the Tide?

Well, we're just a little to the left of that.

They say tourists used to visit our town from time to time, but I find that hard to believe. Deeper Harbour couldn't attract tourists if we built our own fantasy theme park and advertised free rides on flying dinosaurs.

Not even before they built that new highway.

You see, Deeper Harbour doesn't have much in the way of tourist attractions. In fact, it doesn't have anything at all. We've got a pizza shop that specializes in salt cod and pork scraps. We don't have a McDonald's. We don't have a movie theatre. We don't have anything at all but a complete lack of expectations.

Hypothetically speaking, I could be exaggerating how bad things really are in Deeper Harbour, except I couldn't spell the word hypothetically if I gargled a bucket of alphabet soup while chewing on a dictionary sandwich. The fact is that life in Deeper Harbour isn't really as bad as I'm telling you.

It's a whole lot worse.

So when Warren Boudreau, Dulsie's dad, stomped into the police station in a bathrobe, jeans, and a pair of fuzzy brown sasquatch slippers, I wasn't the least bit surprised.

"You sure didn't waste any time getting here," Dad said.

"It was a lucky thing I was sitting by the phone at three in the morning just waiting for Molly Winter to tell me some crazy man in a kilt had thrown a stolen clothesline pole straight through my only dory."

Warren kept on complaining, only stopping for breath every three or four rants, while Dad sat down at his desk and rummaged through the drawer. I watched closely as Dad fished out a pair of earplugs and worked them into his ears.

Meanwhile, Granddad Angus propped the saw between his feet and chin, leaning on it until the blade bent into a giant letter S, and began tuning up a rendition of "Farewell to Nova Scotia" on his musical saw, using a small homemade bow that he had previously constructed from fishing line and a small wooden ruler. He'd pulled the bow from out of his many-pocketed fishing vest.

"You let him keep the saw?" Warren asked.

"And a file too," Dad answered. "I'm waiting for him to try to escape before I shoot him in the kneecaps a couple of times."

Granddad Angus was far too busy making his own particular brand of music to notice all of that divinely inspired sarcasm. There is nothing that sounds quite so weird as a musical saw, all deep and moonish and eerie, as if someone were drowning a giant mutant screech owl in the belly of a kettle drum about a thousand miles beneath the ocean.

A vein on Warren's forehead swelled up and pulsed in harmony with the caterwaul saw. It looked a little like a radioactive caterpillar had crawled beneath his skin and was giving birth to the Loch Ness Monster while sumo wrestling with Godzilla, which—

BANG!

My mom, the mayor of Deeper Harbour and the woman divorcing my dad, walked in and slammed the door behind her.

The whole room shook for a minute before becoming quiet.

"Take those earplugs out of your ears," Mom said to Dad without missing a beat.

Dad yanked the earplugs out as if his earwax had caught fire.

"I didn't do anything," I said, which was how I started most conversations with Mom.

"Your son wrecked my dory," Warren said, pointing at me. It didn't sound like he'd figured out Dulsie was part of our caber caper yet—and that was probably for the best.

"He had help, you know," Granddad Angus butted in.

"Warren, I can't remember the last time I saw you out in that dory," Mom said.

"I was saving it for when the tourists came back," Warren explained, looking hurt. "I figured I could give rowing tours of the harbour. Tourists are just hungering for that sort of cultural experience."

Hungering?

I giggled, picturing a horde of undead zombie tourists stumbling off a rusty black bus, their arms stuck out Frankenstein-straight, moaning for brains, postcards, and t-shirts.

"Warren, you have got to stop reading those tourism brochures," Mom said, shaking her head sadly. "Your boat shed and the old wharf are both nearly ready to tip over into the sea. They should have been torn down years ago."

Then she turned to Granddad Angus. "It's a good thing you're so handy with that saw of yours—since you seem to be responsible for sinking Warren's dory, you can drag it up to the shore and help Warren patch it."

Granddad Angus didn't like that. Neither did Warren.

"I don't want that man anywhere near my dory," Warren said.

"I don't remember asking your opinion," Mom said, turning to look at Dad. "Have you told your son what we've been talking about?"

Dad didn't say a word. He looked down at the floor. I think he was wishing he'd kept his earplugs plugged in.

Mom looked at me.

"What?" I asked, trying hard to keep that you-know-what tone out of my voice.

"I'm going to get your father to unlock this cell and let you go free."

That was good news.

"I want you to take the time this summer and play just as hard as you can."

Also good news.

"I want you to spend as much time with your father and your grandfather as you can. I also want you to help your grandfather patch up Warren's dory…because by the end of the summer you and I are leaving Deeper Harbour. We're moving to Ottawa."

Leaving?

All of a sudden everyone started talking at once.

"But I don't want to leave," I said.

"You'll love Ottawa," Mom assured me.

"I grew up in this town," Dad said. "So did you. Roland should too."

"What about my dory?" Warren wanted to know.

"Are you still here?" Mom asked, giving Warren a look.

Warren opened his mouth, thought better of it, and closed it up again. He turned and shuffled out of the police station, his furry sasquatch slippers leading the way.

"This town is dying," Mom said. "There's nothing here to see. There's nothing here to do. There's no future for a boy Roland's age."

"That's fine talk for the mayor," Granddad Angus said.

"I was a mom long before I was a mayor," Mom said. "You wouldn't have gotten into the kind of trouble you did tonight if you had been living in a city where there was more to do than just get into trouble."

"I was having fun," I said.

Except Mom wasn't listening to me.

"I'm resigning from my position as mayor," she said. "I'll give proper notice at the council meeting next week."

"Mayors can't resign," Dad said.

"Watch me," Mom replied. "I've already taken a job in Ottawa."

"But I don't want to go to Ottawa," I said.

Except nobody was listening to me.

"I'll fight you in court," Dad said, drawing the threat like a line in the dirt.

I had heard Mom and Dad fight a lot these last two years and even back before they thought of divorce, so I should have been used to this sort of arguing. Still, a fourteen-year-old kid doesn't like to hear his parents going tug-of-war on him like he's a bone caught between two stray dogs.

"You'll lose," Mom said to Dad. "Look at you. You're keeping him locked in a jail cell, for heaven's sake."

Dad didn't have any kind of answer to that one.

"Get packed and come home," Mom said to me. "I'll be expecting you for breakfast."

Then she turned away and slammed the door behind her.

BANG—clack.

Dad got up and walked slowly to the freshly slammed door.

He took a deep breath—and then kicked it down.

BLAMMM! Right off the hinges.

Granddad Angus kicked his saw across the floor of the jail cell. It made a bow-wowing-tin-roof-explosion sort of sound—not half as noisy as kicking down a door, but with a lot more echo. The saw wobbled across the cell floor, fell with a clatter, and lay there like a set of giant robot dentures. I didn't have anything to kick so I stood there feeling like someone had slammed a door in my face about ten thousand times.

My heart sank deeper than the bottom of the sea, sank about two miles deeper than that, drowned a little, and continued to sink on down. I just sat there, listening to the silence that hung on a long time after the door-slam and the door-kick and the saw-fall had died away.

And that was it. That's the sound that scared me more than anything in my whole life. Not the cell lock clicking shut, not the kicked-down door, not even the howl of the caterwaul saw. That silence hanging on long after the thunder of Mom's wordless good-bye was the single scariest sound I had ever heard.

Life had gone and changed.

Suddenly.

Chapter 5

SNAKE SECRETS

There's always a scene in those old Coyote and Road Runner cartoons where something heavy like an anvil or a piano or the CN Tower is falling towards that old Coyote's head and he takes the time to open up a teeny-tiny umbrella and squint his eyes like he knows it's going to hurt and there isn't a thing he can do about escaping that hurt except hold up a teeny-tiny umbrella and wait—which was how I felt knowing that Ottawa was about to drop on my head. Only I didn't even own an umbrella.

Dad unlocked the cell door.

"Go on home," he said.

Granddad Angus picked up his saw, re-pocketed his bow, and walked through the kicked-down door, not saying a word.

Neither of them looked at each other.

Now who was moping?

Then Dad spoke to me.

"I guess I can't hold you here," was what he said, which, translated, means "Mom wins again."

Mom always wins. That's how she went from being a school-teacher to being the mayor of Deeper Harbour. That's what happened when she told Dad that they needed a divorce, just the same way she might have said that they needed a new can opener. Mom always wins—and as much as I love her because she is my mom, right then I also hated her just as much as a fourteen-year-old could hate anything in his life.

Feelings are a little like an ocean that way.

They are deep and can flow in a whole lot of directions.

"You probably ought to go home," Dad told me. "This police station is apt to be a little drafty until I get this door patched up."

I thought about that.

Actually, I had been thinking non-stop since Mom laid down her news.

I knew I ought to stay here and help Dad clean up the mess. I knew there was no way on earth that I wanted to see Mom right now, much less join her for breakfast, but I kept thinking about how she'd said there were no tourists and no future in Deeper Harbour. I kept thinking about how she'd said there was nothing to see here. I kept thinking about how Granddad Angus had said we'd given Deeper Harbour something to look at when we wrecked the dory and I kept thinking about Warren's radioactive mutant vein and I kept thinking about how that caber looked, poking out of the boat.

I kept thinking there had to be something I could do about this mess—but "Okay, Dad," was all I said.

And then I ran for home, following the distant compass of my mother's footsteps, which had vanished down the same street that Granddad Angus and I had run along just an hour earlier with a clothesline-pole caber. I ran, feeling the spring of the dirt that slept beneath the pavement of the street. I ran, allowing my sneakered feet to beat the street as if somehow I could run all of my problems to death.

I ran, full out, all go, with no stop, kicking one foot out after the other, following a trail that only my toes seemed to know—hoping that somewhere between the right-now of my dad and the we'll-see of my mother, I would run myself into some sort of a plan.

And halfway home I tripped over an idea.

I was standing in the halo of the hardware store sodium lamp. A big fat garter snake slithered out from under a bush and slid directly in front of my feet. You see a lot of those snakes that time of the year so it didn't scare me. I stopped and watched it move towards a puddle. I think the snake believed that if it could get into the water it would be safe from the dangerous, looming, fourteen-year-old predator that was casting a sodium lamp shadow over it—namely, me.

I watched the snake slither through the puddle like a tiny escalator set on its side, its flat, wedge-shaped head poking up like a periscope. The snake's green and grey and yellow scales rippled and bulged and then it turned and looked up at me as if it was deciding whether to eat me or greet me.

It stuck its tongue out at me at exactly the moment that the idea that had been sneaking around the basement of my imagination jumped up and smacked me directly between the eyes.

I knew just exactly what I needed to do.

Chapter 6

SEA MONSTER SEEDS

Mom sat at the kitchen table like a stack of unavoidable homework. "You ought to eat," she told me.

I peanut-butter-and-jammed some bread, because I did not want to wait for the toast to pop. Mom said a few more things. I nodded back a few times, like I was really listening, yawning between every nod until Mom finally told me that I'd better go to my bedroom and have a nap—which was exactly what I'd planned.

Only I wasn't going to sleep.

I sat on my bed and leaned back with my laptop balanced on my legs, enjoying the perfect groove I'd worn into the mattress over the years. I wondered if I could multiply the years since cribdom and subtract the nights I'd spent out in my tent in the summer and the few times I'd visited our Uncle Wilfred's place to figure out just how much time I'd spent right here—but who in their right mind wants to do math this early in the morning?

I wondered if I would be allowed to take my bed to Ottawa with me.

How much stuff could I bring?

Would I need to get used to sleeping in a brand-new bed?

It didn't matter. I needed to stop feeling sorry for myself. None of that mattered now that I had a plan.

I started out by searching "sea monster" on Google, which brought me about 14,600,000 hits, which wasn't quite a kajillion but close enough. This was going to be harder than I'd thought. So I tried "Canadian sea monster," which narrowed my hunt down to 250,000 results.

I spent an hour rooting my way through the deep heaps of sea monster information I'd discovered. It turned out that Canada was home to an awful lot of monsters: Ogopogo and the Cadborosaurus in British Columbia; another Ogopogo in Alberta; something called Agopogo in Saskatchewan; a Manipogo in Manitoba; Champ in Lake Champlain, Quebec; and Igopogo in Lake Simcoe, Ontario. Further east in New Brunswick was Gougou in Chaleur Bay and Old Ned in Lake Utopia; Okiepogo in O'Keefe Lake, Prince Edward Island; and Cressie in Newfoundland. There were sea monster sightings all around Nova Scotia, including lake lizards in Cranberry Lake and Lake Ainslie, and even monsters spotted right in the middle of Halifax Harbour.

It seemed as if the waters out there were as thick as chowder when it came to sea monsters.

I started taking notes.

Sure, I know that sounds way too much like homework, but I'd decided that I was going to be organized about this. So I made a list of the common elements of every sea monster sighting I'd found.

SEA MONSTERS
— usually spotted in the early morning, or early evening
— fog always helps
— have long necks and short heads
— look a little like a plesiosaurus
— often have a red mane
— need to have "pogo" in the name
— make scary sounds
— sometimes smell funny

I decided to send an email to every sea monster organization and scientific expert I could find to let them know that something huge was happening in Deeper Harbour. Sooner or later, if I talked to enough people, somebody would listen. There'd be stories in the newspaper and on TV. The Deeper Harbour sea monster would get everyone talking.

If there were a sea monster in Deeper Harbour the tourists would come back. Once the tourists came back, the money would come back. Stores would open up and this town would have a real future. Maybe there would be television specials and maybe even an action movie and Mom would say something like, "Hey, why did I ever think we needed to move to Ottawa when there is so much happening right here in Deeper Harbour?"

Yeah, right.

It sounded good in the way that ideas a fourteen-year-old's plan-making muscles come up with can, but who was I kidding? No one would listen to a kid like me.

Still, I had to do something and this was better than doing nothing at all.

It was like planting seeds in a garden. You never know which one will grow.

I added "organizations" to my search and started getting the kind of results I was looking for. I made a list of email addresses for the organizations I found.

I set up an anonymous email address.

I drafted a letter.

I'm telling you, I was organized.

And then I decided exactly who I wanted to email first. It came to me like a thunderbolt to Frankenstein's lightning-attracting neck bolts. I needed to notify the single greatest Canadian scientist that ever lived.

I found his email address on his website.

This would be perfect.

From: deeperharbourmonster@gmail.com
To: David Suzuki

DEAR DAVID SUZUKI,

EARLY LAST NIGHT MY FRIENDS AND I SAW A HORRIBLE SEA MONSTER RIGHT HERE IN THE WATERS OF DEEPER HARBOUR, NOVA SCOTIA. IT HAD A LONG PLESIOSAURUS-LIKE NECK AND A BRIGHT RED MANE AND IT HAD TEETH AND EYES THAT GLOWED IN THE DARK. IT MADE A HORRIBLE SOUND LIKE IT WAS ANGRY OR MAYBE IT WAS LONELY. I DON'T KNOW IF ITS NAME ENDED IN POGO OR NOT BUT I AM WRITING TO YOU IN HOPES THAT YOU WILL COME AND DISCOVER THIS SEA MONSTER. PLEASE SEND THIS EMAIL TO AS MANY PEOPLE AS YOU KNOW.

I BELIEVE IN YOU.

SIGNED: ANONYMOUS

P.S. THE SEA MONSTER SMELLED FUNNY TOO.

All right, I never said I was any kind of a writer. But I thought I'd hit the necessary details. I thought the phrase, "I believe in you" was a pretty good guilt-trip mechanism, and believe you me, nobody understands guilt trips like the fourteen-year-old child of divorcing parents.

I added the GPS coordinates for Deeper Harbour, a map, and a picture of a fishing boat from a Nova Scotia tourism website, then sent my message off. My next step was to send a copy of the email to every monster-hunting organization I had found.

My figuring was pretty simple. If I sent twenty emails to twenty organizations, and they forwarded my email to twenty people, sooner or later my email would have reached every single potential tourist in Canada.

Sending the emails was easy once I fell into a routine, just cut and paste and send, over and over. I wondered if I could get a job doing this sort of thing. Kind of like a publicist for sea serpents and wood beasts across the country.

I wondered if Bigfoot had ever thought of hiring a personal public relations consultant.

I sent a few more messages before erasing the history on my computer just in case Mom got into one of her snooping moods. I closed the laptop and I decided that after being up for most of the night throwing cabers and sinking dories, a half-hour nap would do me just fine.

Three hours later, I was still snoring softly with drool running down my chin when my first reply came winging back to me.

PART II

THE BIRTH OF A SEA MONSTER

Chapter 7

A CHAPTER FOR SKIPPING

The ten-o'clock-in-the-morning sunshine pushed aside my bedroom blinds, pried my eyelids open, and slapped me awake. I rolled out of bed and checked my email. I danced a little dance of yippee-yahoo when I saw that someone had replied to one of my sea monster messages. I read it, tossed my laptop into my backpack, and got going.

I hopped downstairs for my second breakfast of the day. I greased toaster waffles in butter, drowned them in syrup, and forked them down fast. I swallowed a bucket and a half of cold, white milk, thinking chocolate thoughts, and even managed a fake, cheery "Hi Mom," before running out the door. I headed for the harbour.

And so, I guess, had everyone else.

It looked like half of Deeper Harbour was standing on the rickety old wharf staring at the damage we'd done. I expected the other half of Deeper Harbour's population was checking out Molly's desecrated pumpkin patch.

I found Dulsie and Granddad Angus standing in the shadow of Warren's boat shed. Dulsie was wearing a battered straw hat that looked too beat up for any self-respecting scarecrow to be caught dead wearing it. A scrap of fishing net hung off the hat and over her face.

"What's the net for?" I asked.

"It's a veil," Dulsie explained. "I'm in mourning. Don't you see the tears?"

I looked closer and saw that she had painted big black tears down her cheeks.

"What are you mourning for?" I asked.

"This town," Dulsie said. "My dad told me what your mom said when he got home from the police station."

"What about it?" I asked.

"Your mom is right," Dulsie said. "This town is dying."

No, it isn't, I thought. I had the answer to all of our troubles, only I didn't want to tell her just yet so I bent down and picked up a stone and skipped it across the water.

Skip—skip—skip—sploosh.

Dulsie bent down and picked up a stone of her own—a nice flat spinner. She sidearmed it with just the right amount of flick at the end of her throw. I wouldn't want to admit it, but she threw a whole better than I did.

Skip—skip—skip—skip—skip—sploosh.

"That's a pretty good throw," Granddad Angus said.

"Ha," somebody said from behind us, "it runs in the family."

I turned around. It was Warren, with a stone of his own in his hand. For a moment, I was afraid he was going to throw it at me.

"You're out awfully early," he said to Dulsie.

"I couldn't sleep," she said.

"Your mom was that way," Warren said. "You are just the same as she was."

Dulsie's mom had died in a car wreck eight years ago, when Dulsie was seven years old. She says it doesn't bother her anymore, but I kind of wonder about that. There is some paint that will never wash off.

"Am not," Dulsie said and Warren let the argument lie.

He took two steps forward and skipped his own stone out across the water.

Skip—skip—skip—skip—skip—skip—skip—clunk.

Whoops.

The *clunk* was the sound of Warren's stone smacking against the bottom of his caber-impaled dory. I expected him to get angry at the reminder of how Granddad and I had damaged his boat, but Warren just laughed.

"I guess it's a good thing that dory was wrecked," he said. "I've been hanging on to the hope that our tourism would return, but let's face it—the mayor is right."

I was getting sick and tired of hearing how right Mom was. She had taken the wind out of Warren's sails, just that easily, and that bugged me. It didn't help that I was afraid that maybe she was right.

"I think I'm just going to leave that dory floating out there," Warren went on. "Kind of like a tombstone to a town that went and died."

Enough was enough.

"Want to bet?" I said. "This town isn't ready to die just yet."

"I've got two words for you," Warren said. "Im—possible."

That's when I told them about my plan. I pulled out my laptop and showed them the email I'd gotten that morning.

To: deeperharbourmonster@gmail.com
From: Dreamchasers

Hi there, anonymous.

I got your email and your story sounds fascinating. As Canada's premier cryptid hunting society I feel I might have to get involved and investigate this phenomenun. Can you give me any more details than you have offered? Have there been any photographs taken? Is there a history of cryptid sightings in your town? Has anyone else besides you seen this creature? Can you give me your name?

"A sea serpent?" Warren said.

"That email is a start, I guess," Granddad Angus said. "Even though he did misspell the words 'premiere' and 'phenomenon.'"

"And I'm not that crazy about how he uses the words 'society' and 'I' in the same sentence," Warren pointed out. "It sounds to me as if we might be dealing with a society of one person."

"And where are we going to get photographs?" Dulsie asked.

"All we need to do is spread a few more rumours," I said. "It's like spreading a cold. Sneeze on enough people and you create an epidemic. I bet there'll be television crews and newspaper articles and we'll have tourists coming out of our ears."

"Is that what you figure?" Warren asked.

"The boy is on to something," Granddad Angus said. "Just look at all these people come out to stare at a caber-impaled dory. People always come when there's something to look at."

"So?" Warren asked.

"What about the Shag Harbour UFO crash back in 1967? That

was in newspapers and books, too. Tourists still go there, hoping for a glimpse of a flying saucer."

"Shediac has a giant lobster," Dulsie added. "People go see that."

"And Sydney has a giant fiddle," I put in.

"Nackawic in New Brunswick has a giant axe," Granddad Angus went on, "and Stewiacke has a giant mammoth."

"A mammoth what?" Warren asked.

"A big elephant that needs a haircut," Granddad Angus explained. "All Deeper Harbour needs is an attraction, just like that one."

He pointed out at Warren's dory.

"We don't need to build anything at first," he said. "That's the beauty of it. We can start with a legend. It's like all those old ghost stories people keep telling around campfires—if enough people tell a story long enough, it grows its own form of true."

"Like the Boy Scout ghosts of Muddy Lake," Dulsie said.

"That's right," Granddad Angus said.

"Or like the Loch Ness Monster," she said.

"That's right again, girl, like Loch Ness. If we spread the word that there's a sea monster out there," Granddad Angus said, pointing out the harbour, "then the tourists will come."

"Nobody will believe it," Warren said.

"Like Roland said, do you want to bet?" Granddad Angus asked. "Why don't you try to out-skip me? If you lose you have to agree to help me and the kids spread a sea monster story."

"I'm not betting with you," Warren said.

"Why not?" I asked. "Are you chicken?"

"He is," Dulsie said. "My dad is a big chicken."

Granddad Angus poked his fists into his armpits and began

scratching the toes of his sneakers in the dirt, bucking his neck back and forth and looking as if someone had wrapped a kilt around the biggest, ugliest Rhode Island Red rooster in the world.

"Buck, buck, buckaw," Granddad Angus clucked. "Buck, buck, buckaw."

There is something both irritating and irresistible about the sight of a thousand-year-old man in a kilt making chicken sounds while doing a funky chicken dance. It gets under your skin and worms away at your common sense like a gigantic double-dare.

"That's a lot to ride on the fling of a stone," Warren argued.

I started clucking as well. Dulsie joined in too.

"All right," Warren said. "You've got yourself a bet."

He stooped for another stone and winged it.

Skip—skip—skip—skip—skip—skip—skip—skip—skip—skip—skip—skip—skip…sploosh.

"Ha!" Warren laughed. "Thirteen skips. I guess you lose."

Wow.

I had no idea that Warren Boudreau was a world-champion, gold-medal, Olympic-class stone skipper. Granddad Angus didn't seem to be worried, though. He calmly rooted a stone from out of his magic fishing vest of many pockets.

"Do you see this stone?" he asked, holding up what looked to be a perfectly ordinary, flat, triangular shard of slightly blackened beach stone. "This used to be a Mi'kmaq arrowhead. Long before we started writing history down, an ancient hunter tracked a rare white deer down to the shoreline and sent this arrowhead straight through the deer's beating heart."

Warren, Dulsie, and I stood there listening and thinking. It was a gift that Granddad Angus had. When he started spinning those words it was like the world's largest 3-D television went on somewhere in the back of your brain.

"The hunter sang a song," Granddad Angus went on, "a song so beautiful that the wind stopped blowing and the tide stopped turning and even the seagulls came down to listen. And then he threw the arrowhead stone into the water. Several centuries later, the stone washed ashore and I picked it up and put it in my pocket."

"That's just a story," Warren said.

"Doesn't mean it isn't true," Granddad Angus argued. "If you tell a story long enough and hard enough it becomes true."

"So why didn't he keep the arrowhead?" Warren asked.

"Because the arrowhead had done its job already," Dulsie said.

"Right you are," Granddad Angus said. "The arrowhead had made its flight and done its magic and the Mi'kmaq chief knew that he had to return the stone to the sea."

"There's no such thing as magic," Warren said.

"Says you," Granddad Angus retorted. "This is the stone of fly-far."

"Says who?" Warren asked.

"Says me," Granddad Angus replied. "And who can say any differently?"

When someone makes a claim as bold as that there is only one thing you can do.

"Prove it," Warren, Dulsie, and I said tri-multaneously.

Granddad Angus just grinned at the three of us.

"Magic grows wild on the beach, here in Nova Scotia," he told us. "Never doubt it for a heartbeat."

And then Granddad Angus let the stone fly free.

Skip—skip—skip—skip—skip—skip—skip—skip—skip—

skip—skip—skip—skip—skip—skip—skip—skip—skip—skip—
skip—skip—skip—skip—skip—skip—skip—skip—skip...

The stone of fly-far skimmed and skipped off into the distance, further than I could ever hope to see. Part of me wondered if maybe the stone had splashed into the water and I'd blinked and missed it. Another part wondered if the wind hadn't somehow taken the stone and blown it farther than it should have, but the deepest, quietest, stillest part of me wondered if somehow Granddad Angus hadn't thrown that stone far beyond the farthest lip of the horizon and deep into the heart of forever.

"So where are we going to come up with a sea monster?" Warren asked.

"Right out there," Granddad Angus said, pointing at Warren's dory. "All we need is a good strong rope and enough backbone to drag that dory up to the shed."

Chapter 8

HEAVING THE DORY

"HEAVE!"

The four of us—Granddad Angus, Warren, Dulsie, and me—leaned, hauled, muckled, bore down, and came a daisy onto about a million and a half pounds of dory and clothesline-pole caber after Warren had finished fishing the mooring rope up out of the water.

"Wouldn't it be easier to just rent a tow truck?" I asked.

"Keep pulling," Granddad Angus ordered.

"We could have hired a helicopter," I suggested, "or taken a fishing boat out and towed the dory in."

"Where would be the fun in that?" Granddad Angus asked.

"Heave!" Warren shouted again.

I heaved. The rope quivered, shook, and burned in the palms of my hands like a two-hundred-foot-long electric eel. I wondered if there would be time to go home and get five or six pairs of work gloves from the basement and put them on, slowly, one at a time, while I watched everybody but me heave up that one-and-a-half-million-pound dory.

"Heave!"

I squeezed my eyes closed.

I was certain I would have a heart attack any minute now and puke my guts out and my head would explode. Then, when I opened my eyes the rope had grown two more pairs of hands as a couple of onlookers grabbed hold. The dory grew a little lighter.

"Heave!" Warren and Granddad Angus said together.

So I heaved, and as I heaved I kept my eyes on the waves beating against the rocks. I wondered how long those waves had washed this bit of shoreline. It felt good watching those waves splash the stones. They never changed. They just kept washing ashore, always reaching and never quite making it. There really isn't a place in town you can stand without hearing waves on rock.

If the waves didn't change maybe nothing else really needed to change. Maybe I wouldn't have to go to Ottawa. Maybe I could stay in Deeper Harbour.

It was something to hang on to while I heaved.

I can do this.

If I can drag a dory and a caber out of the harbour then maybe, just maybe, I can make a sea monster.

The rope grew a few more pairs of hands.

The dory was flying through the water like a speedboat.

We heaved it ashore, hauled it into the boat shed, and set it on a pair of sawhorses that looked old enough to have stood in Noah's very first ark-building shop. After that, all of the people who'd helped us wandered down to the tavern to talk over the amazing feat they'd accomplished—namely, hauling up our dory.

That's how a town works, I guess.

"So when do we build the sea monster?" I asked.

"One step at a time," Granddad Angus said. "First, I figure you and Dulsie should go and get started on patching up Molly's pumpkin patch."

"But I want to help," I said.

"First the pumpkin patch," Granddad Angus said.

I might have known.

That's how grown-ups work. Every time they are building something interesting and you want to help they send you off for a screwdriver, and by the time you get back with the screwdriver the whole thing is done.

"Why does Dulsie have to help?" Warren asked.

Apparently, Warren still didn't know that Dulsie had been part of our midnight caber toss, which was good. Warren seemed okay with the idea of us smashing his dory, but I wasn't sure how he'd feel if he found out that Dulsie was involved. Parents can be awfully peculiar when it comes to their kids.

"Getting these kids out of the way will give us time to figure out a plan," Granddad Angus said.

"I'm not going anywhere near that old bat Molly," Dulsie said. "She can kiss my ripe, rosy, Maritime—"

"DULSIE!" Warren yelled, cutting her off just in time.

She turned, giggled just a little, and then ran in the other direction.

I guess I was on my own.

I plodded off to go dig my own grave in Molly's garden.

Chapter 9

THE TASTE OF LEMONADE AND DIRT

I eased Molly's front gate open.

The gate should have squeeeeaaaked like Dracula's coffin directly before he jumps out and spreads his bat wings and suction-fangs you right in the neck—only it didn't. I guess Molly Winter wasn't Dracula—or else she'd found the time to oil up that gate.

"Are you going to stand there all day or come on in?"

It was Molly, of course.

"You and your granddad sure made a mess out here," Molly said. "The pumpkin patch is nearly ruined."

I felt bad about that.

"Your granddad was always a few pea pods short of a tuna casserole," Molly said, shaking her head sadly. "But I thought you would know better."

"That's not true," I argued. "Granddad Angus has an imagination, is all. What in the world would a librarian know about imagination?"

Molly just laughed.

"Imagination, eh? I guess that's one word for it. He always was a deep one," she argued back.

I was supposed to be polite. After all, I had been the one who had wrecked her garden, stolen her clothesline pole, and knocked down her fence.

"I've got a garden to dig," I said, because it was safer than arguing with her.

I took the shovel that she handed me and went out back to the garden.

The pumpkins were a total write-off. She'd need a new clothesline pole. I'd need Granddad's help to fix the fence, too. So I settled for scooping up the pumpkins and dumping them in the compost heap.

When I was tired of shovelling, I watched a fat earthworm twisting and wriggling deeper and deeper into the fresh-turned dirt. I had the funny feeling that my answer was down there, buried in the darkness—the whole sea monster, buried with the worms and bugs. I was thinking about sea monsters and looking at that worm when Molly came up behind me and touched the back of my neck.

I only jumped a little.

"Come on," she said. "You've worked hard enough. I've mixed some lemonade."

The lemonade tasted pretty good, as I sat and sipped on Molly's front porch swing.

"You're scared of leaving Deeper Harbour, aren't you?" Molly asked.

Scared?

"Yes," I said. "I'm scared."

I sipped a bit more lemonade.

"It's just dirt," Molly finally said. "That's all Deeper Harbour is, just the same as Ottawa. Just think of yourself as being like that worm digging in the dirt. He doesn't know what's down there so he digs just deep enough to see where he is supposed to be next."

"You're telling me that Ottawa is a hole?"

I knew that already, deep down inside.

"I'm telling you that Ottawa is nothing more than a city built on Deeper Harbour dirt. It's all connected—the dirt your roots grew up in and the dirt you're moving towards. The wind blows and the seed travels and something new will grow out of something old."

I nodded like I understood what she was trying to tell me.

"You can't hang on to dirt," Molly said. "All you can carry is memories and stories and dreams."

Old folks say some awfully foolish things.

"Sip on that lemonade," Molly told me. "It's sweet, isn't it? It tastes of sunshine and rain and puckered kisses. Yet the lemons that were squeezed to make that lemonade grew up in dirt and manure and were fed on sunshine and rain and whatever the worm left behind."

I looked at her like she had suddenly begun speaking in Swahili.

"It takes all kinds of weather to make a good glass of lemonade," Molly went on. "It takes dirt and manure and worms. You'll find something sweet in Ottawa, I guarantee, no matter how hard it feels to uproot."

Enough was enough.

"I could have stayed at home and watched Oprah if I'd wanted to hear a sugar-coated sermon," I said. "You don't have a clue what I'm going through."

"I'm afraid I do, Roland McTavish."

"How's that?"

She drew in a long, deep sigh that sounded a little like the waves sliding away from the rocks.

"I have to leave my home too," Molly said. "Or else it's leaving me."

I looked around at her house and yard.

"Don't you own this?"

"That's not what I'm talking about. This isn't my home. This is just where I live. My home is in that school library and they're closing it down."

"They're closing the library?" I asked.

"They're closing the whole school," she said. "They're busing the students to a school in Yarmouth."

Then she stood up and walked back into the house, leaving the glass of lemonade, half-finished, on the porch. Which was where I left my glass, half-finished, when I got up to walk home. Mom must have known about the school closing. She's the mayor. That must have been one of the reasons she decided to move to Ottawa.

I had to do something.

I had to save this town.

I spat once.

It tasted of lemonade and dirt.

Chapter 10

FEEDING A COLD

Dulsie's today tattoo was a giant green crocodile with a jawbone that she'd stretched down under her chin and onto the hollow of her chest bones, so that when she raised her chin and kept her mouth closed it looked like she was wearing a giant, open mouth. Being Dulsie, she never kept her mouth closed long enough for the illusion to properly take effect.

"Guess what?" she asked. "I joined your group."

"Group?" I said. I wasn't sure that Granddad Angus and I qualified as a group.

"On Facebook. Your sea monster group. I joined."

Dulsie pulled out her laptop and showed me the Facebook page.

"I didn't do this," I said, kind of wishing I had. "Who set this up?"

"I don't know," Dulsie said with a shrug. "Somebody set it up using a fake name."

"How do you know it's a fake name?" I asked. "A lot of people have strange names."

"You've met somebody named Seethe C. Monster, have you?" Dulsie asked.

"Well, you never know," I argued, even though I didn't really believe it myself.

So far, the group had 382 members. They were calling our monster "Fogopogo, the beast of Deeper Harbour." Fogo was an island just off of the northern coast of Newfoundland, a long way away from Deeper Harbour. Still, at least they got the "pogo" right.

"Who would do this?" I asked. "Do you think it could be your dad?"

Dulsie laughed at that.

"My dad thinks that computers are the cause of global warming," Dulsie said. "He really doesn't trust them. He's a diehard stamp collector and I think he resents the idea that email will replace postage stamps."

"A stamp collector?" I said.

I had never known that about Warren before.

"It's a dad thing, I think," Dulsie said. "Maybe your grandfather did this?"

I looked at the screen again. I tried to picture Granddad Angus setting up a Facebook page, which was even harder to believe in than a sea monster. As far as Granddad Angus was concerned, websites were somewhere spiders hung out.

"I don't think so," I said.

"Well, somebody started it," Dulsie said.

It could have been anyone. Ever since we'd decided to give Deeper Harbour a sea monster, word had really gotten around. Warren had talked to his dart team and Granddad Angus had been telling sea monster stories over at the church bingo hall. I'd heard people talking about sea monster sightings at Nora's Diner, too. Spreading rumours really was like spreading a cold, and we were sneezing on more people every day.

"That's nothing," I said. "The Deeper Harbour police just reported a sea monster in the harbour."

"Your dad saw Fogopogo?"

"Dad didn't see a thing. I waited until he was out of the office to use his email."

"You didn't," Dulsie said, raising her eyebrows.

"I asked his permission," I said.

"You asked his permission to send out a sea monster report?"

"No, I asked his permission to send some emails. He said okay just as long as I didn't download a bunch of games. Which I didn't."

I felt bad lying to Dad, but it was for his own good. If I could get tourists to come to Deeper Harbour, maybe I could stay here with him.

"Is your computer broken?"

"My computer's fine. I just wanted the report to come from somebody with authority."

"Your dad has authority?"

"His email address has authority. I figure if more people spread the word about Fogopogo, then more people are likely to believe in it. And who would be more believable than the chief of police?"

I had sent a message saying that the Deeper Harbour Police Department was flooded with sea monster reports to every address on my list, and made sure the replies would come to my own email address.

"What if he finds out?" Dulsie asked. "Don't you think people will ask him about it?"

"Maybe," I admitted. "But I think he'd have to agree that I'm doing it for a good cause."

"You're sure about that, are you?"

"Mostly sure," I admitted. "More sure of Dad than I am of Mom."

"You've used your mom's email, too?"

"I'm going to. People are bound to listen if they start getting messages from the mayor's office, aren't they?"

"She'll find out, Roland. There's no way she won't find out. She's the mayor, for crying out loud."

"She announced that she's resigning last night," I said. "She's busy worrying about her new job and packing and all that foolishness. Besides, it's her fault for coming up with the idea of moving to Ottawa in the first place."

"She's still your mother," Dulsie said. "And she is the mayor."

"So what? I hate her. And besides, she won't be the town mayor for much longer. I hate her," I repeated.

Dulsie thought about that.

"It seems to me that having any kind of mom beats having a dead one," Dulsie said—and then she closed her mouth and showed me that open-jawed green crocodile tattoo. She turned her back and walked away. I wanted to go after her and tell her I was sorry, but what good would that do?

It couldn't bring her mom back, now could it?

Besides, I really did hate my mom.

Didn't I?

I reminded myself of that fact two hours later when I was standing in Mom's office talking to her.

"Mom?" I asked. "Do you mind if I use your computer?"

I told her the same story I'd told Dad. Mom was just as easy to fool. She felt bad about springing the Ottawa news on me. She left me alone with the computer and I sent more emails—directly from the mayor's office.

Just like spreading a cold—achoo!
Gesundheit.

Chapter 11

THE LUCK OF SEACULLS

It took the four of us nearly two weeks to get the dory back into shape.

Granddad Angus cut the boards with his crosscut saw and Warren used a sheet of plastic and three large steam kettles to make the wood soft enough to bend. After the patching was finished, Dulsie banged in nails while I smoothed the joints with a wood plane. Actually, I tried to smooth the joints, but Dulsie ended up doing that too.

"You make a pretty good carpenter for a girl," I told her.

"Being a good carpenter doesn't have a thing to do with being a girl or a boy," Granddad Angus told me. "You ought to know better than that."

We sealed the joints with goop that smelled a little like the wrong end of a dead moose. Then we painted the dory, which Dulsie liked best of all. To finish it off, we used brushes for the outside and dumped a gallon of red marine paint into the inside and sloshed it around with a mop that Mom might miss someday.

Afterwards, Dulsie and I sat on the wharf and looked out at the harbour.

We watched the waves rolling in and slipping away.

"The ocean is always waving goodbye, isn't it?" Dulsie asked.

"It might be saying hello," I pointed out.

"Might be."

We looked at the water some more.

"Speaking of progress," I said. "I got two more emails. One of them came all the way from Vancouver."

"I phoned the *Chronicle Herald* in Halifax," Dulsie said. "I told them I'd seen the sea monster last week."

"What did they say?" I asked.

"They're going to pass the story on to a reporter who might travel down here to look into it."

"Do you think they'll really send somebody?" I asked.

"I wouldn't hold my breath," Dulsie said. "I know a 'we'll see' when I hear it."

"You never know," I said. "A 'we'll see' can always develop into a 'let me think about it,' which might evolve into a fully grown 'why the heck not?'"

Dulsie giggled at that.

"Keep up the good work," I said.

"I don't know about that," she said. "My dad's awfully worried about his phone bill."

"Tell him he can pay his phone bill with the money he makes giving tourists dory rides."

"Maybe so," she said. "But what if this doesn't work? What if you and your grandfather make this sea monster and your mother still wants to leave?"

"It'll work," I said.

It had to work.

We watched the water some more. A seagull flew overhead and dropped something on my t-shirt. Something that smelled bad.

"Eew," I said, trying to wipe it off.

"Don't do that," Dulsie said. "Mom always said that if a seagull does his business on you it's good luck."

I thought about that.

"It sounds stupid to me," I finally decided.

"It's just something they say, is all," Dulsie said.

"Why do you suppose they say that?" I asked.

"I don't know," Dulsie said. "Maybe they just say it so you won't feel so bad about getting turded on by a seagull."

Then she laughed.

I had to laugh along with her.

I knew that if I did have to go I would miss Dulsie and I knew that Dulsie would miss me. Right now, we were just happy to sit there by the harbour and laugh at each other while the waves kept on washing ashore.

If those waves were saying hello or goodbye, neither of us really cared to notice.

PART III

THE LEGEND GROWS

Chapter 12

INVASION OF THE VENUSIAN VEGAN MONSTER HUNTERS

Remember when I told you about that squadron of wandering Martian death-bots swooping down in a shower of meteors into the middle of a crowded schoolyard and ray-gunning everybody into extinction? Well, they showed up while Dulsie, Dad, and I were sitting in Nora's Diner eating ice cream.

Well, Dulsie was eating ice cream and I was watching mine melt while Dad chowed down on his deep-fried grilled cheese sandwich. He was dunking it in a bowl of homemade tomato soup between mouthfuls, drizzling soup drool and cheese strings down the steel wool tangle of his beard.

I'm not saying it was pretty.

What I'm saying is that all three of us were trying our best not to worry about Ottawa. We each did that in our own kind of way. I didn't feel like eating, so I didn't eat. Dad ate with the single-minded dedication of a grizzly bear getting ready for an ice-age-long hibernation. As for Dulsie, she was there just to eat ice cream and keep an eye on me, which was probably why she had painted an extra eye directly above the bridge of her nose.

Dad was working on his second sandwich when a bright, shiny, purple minivan pulled up in front of the diner.

"Look, Dad," I said. "Tourists."

Dad glanced up at the three strangers walking into Nora's Diner looking as out of place as a carton of eggs at a steamroller convention. The tall one smiled nervously in Dad's direction. He cleared his throat with an honest-to-goodness ahem.

Wow.

I thought that *ahem*-ing only happened in comic books.

"My name's Bertram," the tall one said. He pointed at the man and woman standing beside him. "This is Tim and this is Linda. Are you the town sheriff?"

Sheriff?

"I'm the police chief," Dad said. "Sit down and join us. Nora makes a mean grilled cheese."

"I'm sorry," Bertram said. "But we're vegans."

"Does that mean you aren't allowed to eat sandwiches?" Dad asked.

I knew better than that.

Vegans were people from Venus.

"Being vegan means you avoid anything that comes from animals, like meat or leather," Bertram explained. "We don't eat cheese because it comes from cows."

Whoops.

"Nora cooks a lot more than cheese here," Dad pointed out.

"What kind of oil does she fry with?" Bertram wanted to know.

"WD-40," I said.

"She drains it from her pickup truck every second week or so," Dulsie added.

Bertram looked at us with a sort of bunny-in-the-headlights stare.

I guess vegans aren't big on bad jokes.

"So what are you folks doing in town?" Dad asked.

"We're a team of cryptozoologists," Bertram said in the kind of voice you'd expect a court herald to use while announcing the entrance of the Right Royal Duke of Garlic Calzone. "We investigate legendary and unexplained animals like the yeti, phantom cats, lake monsters, and sea serpents."

Double wow.

Monster hunters.

"You know," Linda said. "Cryptids."

"What's a cryptid?" Dad asked.

"A cryptid is what cryptozoologists study," Tim explained cryptically.

That didn't help much.

"A cryptid is an animal that has been reported to exist but whose existence has yet to be proven," Bertram explained. "The Loch Ness Monster is a cryptid. So is the Alberta lake monster, Ogopogo."

"Oh, you mean like Bigfoot?" Dad asked.

"The proper term is sasquatch," Tim said.

"Don't mind Tim," Linda added. "He's a stickler for detail."

"Actually, I'm a librarian in Halifax," Tim explained. "Bertram is a waiter, and Linda works at Woozles."

Wow.

A cryptozoological Woozle.

"What's Woozles?" Dad asked.

"Only the best children's bookstore in Halifax," Linda said with a quick grin.

"So this is just some sort of a hobby," Dad said.

"Well, there isn't much money in it," Bertram said. "Still, we hope the publicity of this new sighting will help us set up a long-term study. We've put out a press release to newspapers across the province, and TV and radio stations."

Wow to infinity!

A press release!

I tried very hard not to grin. My plan was working. If every monster hunter in Canada sent out enough press releases, sooner or later the tourists would have to start coming to have a look at our sea monster. We'd have tourists and money and a future and Mom would give up on her plan to move us to Ottawa.

Perfect.

"What new sighting?" Dad asked.

"The sighting of the Deeper Harbour sea monster," Bertram said. "We received several reports on our Facebook page."

Several?

"Oh yes," Dad said, nodding knowingly. "It seems to me I've heard talk of something like that."

For some reason, Dad was looking right at me while he said that.

"We'll be setting up a base camp down by the shores of the harbour," Bertram said, "if that's all right with you."

"It's all right by me," Dad said, "if you folks want to tent out on the beach and get chewed up by mosquitoes."

Bertram gave Dad one more of those bunny-in-the-headlights stares before he, Linda, and Tim turned and left.

"Sure hope they see something worth looking at," Dad said.

I looked over at Dulsie. She stared right back at me with all three of her eyes.

"Me too," I said.

Chapter 13

DEAR PRIME MINISTER

It took three days for us to build the frame for the monster out of plastic pipes and chicken wire. Deciding on what Fogopogo should look like took the longest. We wound up with a cross between a mallard duck and a Komodo dragon.

"Time for a break," Warren said. "I want to show you something, Roland."

The two of us sat down in the back room of the boat shed. Warren insisted on making us a pot of tea, even though I would have preferred cocoa.

"Tea is how a Maritimer passes time," Warren explained as he boiled the kettle and fished out the tea bags. "We Maritimers practise our deepest thinking while sitting and waiting for the tea to properly steep."

So we sat and sipped our tea. I wanted badly to find out just what Warren had to show me, but I knew better than to rush him. Besides, I was still thinking about what Dulsie had asked me the other day at the wharf.

What if we made the sea monster and followed through with our plan and my mom still wanted to leave?

"Do you think this is going to work?" I asked him.

"I don't know," Warren answered, "but I'm having the time of my life. I've spent too long waiting for some sort of a sign to show me what to do."

I nodded and sipped my tea, not knowing what else to say.

Warren reached for a pad of paper and a pen and began to write. He peeled the sheet of paper off the pad, crumpled it up, and threw it into the garbage. He began writing again. He got halfway down the page before tearing that one up too.

I had experienced more excitement watching paint dry in the sun, but I didn't want to interrupt Warren's concentration. If I did, he might start all over again and the two of us would be here until several days past infinity.

When Warren was halfway through his third attempt, I couldn't wait any longer. I finally asked, "So what are you writing?"

"A letter to the prime minister," Warren replied, still furiously scribbling. "I'm going to tell him about our sea monster."

"The prime minister of Canada?" I asked. "What are you going to write?"

"I'm telling him that the Deeper Harbour sea monster is an endangered species and that it's his prime ministerial duty to come here and pay his respects."

I had to admit that sounded like a pretty good idea.

"It's not quite David Suzuki and I don't even think the man actually reads his own mail," Warren admitted. "But I just wanted to do something to help."

He sealed the letter up in a huge envelope.

"It just needs the proper stamp, is all."

"Can't you just buy one at the drugstore?" I asked.

"We can't send it with just any old stamp," Warren said. "This is the prime minister of Canada we're talking about. No sir, the choice of a stamp is downright critical."

And then Warren dug out his stamp collection.

Oh my golly. I was pretty sure that staring at Warren's stamp collection might be enough to kill me from sheer boredom.

Only I was wrong. As Warren spread his stamp albums out I began to get interested, in spite of myself. There were stamps of all shapes and sizes; stamps with pictures of spaceships on them; stamps with pictures of dinosaurs; and stamps with pictures of all kinds of strange and wonderful wild animals.

"My own grandfather worked the merchant marine," Warren told me. "He used to send me an envelope full of stamps from whatever port he docked in. After he died I started ordering stamps through the mail."

"Isn't that usually where you get stamps?" I asked. "In the mail?"

"Very funny," Warren said. "I can't tell you how many nights I have spent sitting here at this table, peering at all of these wonderful stamps. Some nights I just sit here and dream about travelling to each of these different countries."

"So why don't you?"

"I don't know," he shrugged. "I've just never gotten around to it, I guess."

I sipped my tea while Warren sorted through his stamps.

"Here," he said. "These will do the trick."

He laid down a block of four shiny Canadian stamps. One had a picture of a werewolf, and the others showed a giant squid, a gorilla, and a sea monster.

Wow.

"That's the Loup-Garou and the Kraken," Warren explained. "And that's Bigfoot and Ogopogo."

"I know Ogopogo," I said. "I read about him on the Internet."

"They're all Canadian monsters," Warren said.

"That's really something," I said. "They're perfect."

"Well, we only need a couple," Warren said.

He carefully selected the Kraken and the Ogopogo stamps. He looked at Ogopogo carefully, as if he were considering something very important. Then he licked the werewolf and Bigfoot stamps and stuck them to the envelope.

"You keep these," he said, handing me the Ogopogo and Kraken stamps.

I tried to give them back.

"You keep them," he repeated. "All these years I've wasted dreaming. Now you come along and bring the stamps to life."

He looked away. He swallowed hard, once or twice.

"I can learn something from you," he told me.

"Me too," I said, which was as profound as my fourteen years allowed me to be.

Chapter 14

HIDE-AND-GO-MOOSE

Fogopogo began to look a little better after Granddad Angus unearthed a nine-hundred-year-old moose hide from somewhere in the back of his garage. The moose hide stank like an old wet basement, and looked more than a little like a prehistoric, zombified, petrified, deep-fried mammoth, but when he laid it over the frame it looked pretty realistic.

"Where did you get this moose hide from?" I asked.

"From a moose, of course. He'd outgrown it. You might say he and his hide came to an unexpected parting of ways."

"Is that the truth?" I asked.

"I'm saying it, aren't I?"

Which didn't help much, but that's all he would tell me as we fastened the moose hide onto the frame. Afterwards, we used a glue gun to stick patches of aluminum foil and plastic wrap onto the moose hide.

"This will catch the light nicely and give it a whole fish-scale sort of look," Granddad Angus explained.

He found some crow feathers that he had been saving in a dried-out paint tin and stitched them to the outside of the hide.

"How's that look?" he asked.

"Like a bunch of black feathers stitched to a smelly old moose hide," Warren said. "Are we fixing on building the world's first flying moose?"

"The feathers will help to break up the silhouette. Just try and imagine seeing it from a distance on a dark and foggy night," Granddad Angus said. "In the end it will look like exactly what people expect to see."

I was more inclined to side with Warren, but I wasn't going to say anything that might spoil the adventure. Even if it didn't work, I was having fun putting this sea monster together.

"The moose hide won't cover the oars," I said. "People will be able to see them."

"We aren't using oars," Granddad Angus said.

"What are we doing then? Swimming?" Dulsie asked.

"The great inventor has a master plan," Warren said. "He won't even tell me about it."

Two days later, Granddad Angus showed us his secret plan.

"Propellers?" Warren said.

A propeller poked through a hole on each side of the dory. They were attached to a set of bike pedals in the centre of the boat. Granddad Angus sat in the dory with his feet on the pedals, and his hands holding on to a pair of handle grips that looked like they had come from a beat-up old bicycle.

My beat-up old bicycle.

"Is that my bicycle?" I asked.

"Well, it was. Now it's something else," Granddad Angus said.

"That was my bike."

"You were figuring on riding that bike to Ottawa, were you?"

Dulsie asked. "Or did you really think your mother would bother to haul your mementos there?"

Mementos?

It is awfully hard to listen to good sense, especially when it is coming to you from the mouth of a fifteen-year-old girl wearing a feather bonnet, with owl eyes painted around her own.

"Life is about letting go of things you no longer need," Granddad Angus explained. "That's how the trees make it through the winter—by letting go of the leaves they no longer need."

Oh sure, I knew the bike was two years too small for me, but I still loved to sit on that purple glitter banana seat in our garage when it rained, reading through my comic book collection.

"They're not propellers," Granddad Angus said. "They're called grinders. You turn the pedal and the grinder turns and moves the boat. They used them on dories that crossed Halifax Harbour back before the ferry boats ever ran."

"Will they work?" Warren asked.

"Like a charm," Granddad Angus said. "They're slow but quiet. They won't make much backsplash. From a distance it'll look like the motion a sea monster would make."

Warren and I nodded doubtfully.

"Besides," Granddad Angus said, lifting a blanket up from the back of the dory, "I put something else in here from that old bike of yours."

I leaned over, had a look, and grinned. Sitting in the stern of the dory, bolted to a sturdy board, was my extra-cushy purple glitter banana seat.

"All right," I said with a grin. "That's more like it."

"We better cut some holes in the moose hide so we can see out of it," Granddad Angus instructed. "And caulk up the seams good and tight. We don't want to sink our sea serpent in the middle of the harbour, do we?"

In the midst of all this excitement I'd somehow forgotten that we planned on sailing this contraption on the open ocean. Thinking about the prospect of sinking made me want to paint and repaint and goop the dory with every kind of waterproofing imaginable.

Now that I thought about it, adding a few life preservers and a Coast Guard helicopter might be a good idea, too.

Chapter 15

A BAD CASE
OF STEGOSAURUS
TURNIP FARTS

The next day, Granddad Angus got us all up earlier than I liked. The crows were still snoring in the trees and a thick and cloying chowder-fog was brewing in the dark harbour.

"There's work to be done," he told me.

I watched as he used a needle that could easily have passed for a whale harpoon to stitch a tangle of yarn onto the dory monster's neck to give it a thick red mane.

"Sea monsters have red manes?" Warren asked.

"It said so in Roland's list of ingredients," Granddad Angus said.

"I think it looks pretty," Dulsie said, which was saying a lot considering she had painted a sunrise across her face. "It needs eyes, I think."

"Right you are," Granddad Angus said, reaching into his magic fishing vest of many pockets and pulling out two glittering chunks of light purple crystal.

"This is amethyst. The Mi'kmaq believed amethyst came to Nova Scotia after young Glooscap scattered his mother's jewellery box across the beach."

"Why would Glooscap do a thing like that?" I asked.

"Why?" Granddad Angus replied. "You might as well ask why oceans grow so deep."

Which didn't tell me much.

"It was probably because he was fourteen years old at the time," Warren suggested. "In a recent Statistics Canada survey, it was proven that every single problem in the universe began with a fourteen-year-old boy."

Dulsie swatted him for that. The swat didn't stop him from giggling, or repeating what he said, or giggling some more, but I think Dulsie enjoyed swatting her dad all the same. As day-old-tea-bag boring as Warren could be sometimes, he sure made a pretty good father for Dulsie.

Granddad Angus glued the amethysts to the sides of Fogopogo's head with a tube of something that smelled strong enough to get up and walk on its own.

"That looks great," Dulsie said. "They glitter, just like a real sea monster's eyes."

"Oh yeah?" Warren asked. "So how many sea monsters have you seen, anyway?"

Dulsie stuck her tongue out at Warren.

"One final detail," Granddad Angus said.

He showed us something that looked like a birch bark dunce's cap.

"What's that for?" I asked.

Granddad Angus barked into the narrow end of the cone in

reply. It made a sound that reminded me of a mutated Labrador retriever.

"It's a moose call," Warren explained. "Hunters use them to call moose."

"Do you think that sounds like a sea monster?"

"Well, what does a sea monster sound like?" Granddad Angus asked.

I had to admit that I had absolutely no idea.

"People believe what they hear," Granddad Angus went on. "So we're going to let them hear a sea monster."

He made a horrifying haroomphing sound with the moose call. It sounded like a bloated stegosaurus with a bad case of turnip farts.

"It's just going to take a bit of practise, is all," Granddad Angus said.

He held the moose call and produced another turnip fart, even stinkier sounding than the last blast.

"Better keep practising," I told him.

Granddad Angus shook his head.

"We're all done with practising," he said. "I think it's time we took our sea monster out for a spin."

Everybody suddenly shut up, the same way that a class full of kids goes silent when a teacher walks into the room. It was one thing to build a sea monster. It was quite another thing to actually sail it on the open sea.

"You really want to take this thing out into the harbour?"

"It's not a thing. It's got a name now. Everybody calls it Fogopogo," Granddad Angus said. "And we're taking Fogopogo out for a dip in Deeper Harbour."

"And how will we get it into the harbour?" Warren asked.

"Simple," Granddad Angus said. "We'll take it out through Muddy Lake."

I swallowed and took a deep breath, enjoying what I was sure would be one of my last.

Chapter 16

MUDDY LAKE MANOEUVRES

Nobody in Deeper Harbour really knows just how deep Muddy Lake is, but it's a fair bet that the bottom is awfully close to for- ever. The lake sits about half a mile out of town and feeds into the ocean just outside of the harbour through a winding stream we call the Drain.

There is a story passed around of a skidoo accident that happened many years ago. It seems a group of Scouts were on an ice-fishing trip. They were scooting across the ice when it cracked open, sending all three of the skidoos to the bottom of the lake. My dad says that it's nothing but an old story that people tell to scare kids away from the thin ice—only Granddad Angus said differently.

"It's a sad, true story," Granddad Angus told me. "The ice opened up like a giant mouth, swallowed them up, and turned them into ice cubes."

True or not, the story is soaked indelibly into the soggy annals of Deeper Harbour history. Kids around here say you can still hear the ghosts of those Scouts howling like wolves and reciting their Cub Scout promises on lonely, full-moon nights.

"Ice is funny that way," Granddad Angus said. "You can look at it and it looks fine, but underneath the surface the rot has set in. The water, deep and warm, eats away at the strength of the ice. Things change, even if you can't see it happening."

And that spot on Muddy Lake was exactly where Granddad Angus wanted to test Fogopogo.

Warren backed his old station wagon, towing a gigantic wooden boat trailer, up to the boat shed. We loaded Fogopogo onto the trailer and covered it up with an industrial-sized tarp held down with some bungee cords and a whole lot of duct tape.

We drove away before the sun came up. I had told Mom that Granddad Angus was taking me fishing. I was getting pretty good at telling lies. I felt bad about that, but Granddad Angus always says that a storyteller needs to be a pretty good liar. Besides, it was nice to be good at something.

"This fog gets any thicker," Warren fussed, "and I'm apt to drive us into the water, dory and all."

"The fog is what we want," Granddad Angus said. "It'll add to the air of illusion. That's why I picked today for the monster test launch."

"Should I go down Main Street?" Warren wanted to know.

"How else are we going to get out of town?" Granddad Angus replied. "Besides, this is Deeper Harbour. Seeing a trailer rolling down Main Street with a boat-sized, tarpaulin-wrapped shape on the back is not going to make anyone raise an eyebrow."

As we rolled down Main Street and past the police station, I thought I saw Dad waving at us. Or maybe I just imagined I saw him. As we got to the end of the street, I looked back. I still thought I could see Dad standing there in front of the police station, waving goodbye to a son running away from home in an old station wagon pulling an ark-sized boat trailer covered in duct tape and plastic. He receded into a dot in the distance, we hit one more bump, and then he was gone.

"What are you looking at?" Granddad Angus asked.

"Nothing," I said.

When we arrived at the shore, the fog was so thick you couldn't see more than ten feet in front of you.

Lowering Fogopogo into Muddy Lake should have been easy. I mean, we had gravity on our side, but it was tougher than I had figured.

"I'd feel safer if it wasn't so close to duck-hunting season," Warren said.

"Most of the hunters around here can't aim worth spit," Dulsie said.

"You better hope so," Warren told her. "What's with that getup of yours?"

Dulsie was dressed all in blue and green with a halo of goose down and the tracing of fish scales across her face and a magnificent sea serpent painted across her neck, up the sides of her face, over her eyebrows, and down the other shoulder. I wasn't sure if she was a bird or fish. The truth was, I wasn't sure if she knew just what she was supposed to be.

"We're fine," Granddad Angus assured us. "Duck-hunting season is weeks away."

"All the same, I'd feel better if this hunting shirt of mine was bulletproof," Warren said.

"Stop your worrying," Granddad Angus told him. "Even if there are any hunters out here bold enough to shoot at a full-grown sea monster, they would most likely miss."

"Maybe so," Warren said. "But I still feel as if I've got 'mallard' written all over my backside."

"Then make like a mallard and duck," I suggested.

Everyone laughed, even Warren.

Then Warren tilted the trailer back and Granddad Angus took hold of his pry bar and me and Dulsie grabbed up a pair of two-by-fours and levered Fogopogo down into the water. The dory monster rolled going down and nearly crushed me against a nearby poplar tree.

"Hang on, Roland," Granddad Angus shouted.

Easy for him to say. He wasn't the one trapped between a tree and Fogopogo. All I smelled was the reek of worked-in mud, lake moss, and prehistoric moose hide. I breathed shallow and slow, trying not to stare directly into Fogopogo's dark amethyst eyes.

I could swallow you up whole was what those eyes were saying to me.

You bet was what I was thinking.

I tried to stay just as calm as I could while Granddad Angus, Warren, and Dulsie pushed Fogopogo clear. The dory monster slid into the water of Muddy Lake. It made a wet swallowing sound as it went, as if the water was somehow digesting the nine-hundred-year-old moose hide.

"Climb in," Warren shouted. "Before it drifts away on us."

So we all dove into the cold, smelly water and clambered underneath the flap in the moose hide. It was darker than a belly full of midnight and twice as scary. I knew just what the dory monster looked like. I'd scraped its hide and smoothed its bones and mopped its guts with cheap red paint, yet something about the dark and the lake and the closeness scared the heck out of me.

At least the pedal-propellers worked fine. Warren worked one and I worked the other. It took more than a few minutes for the two of us to coordinate our efforts. If he turned his pedal too hard or too fast we would swerve in my direction, and if I turned my pedal-propeller too hard we'd spin towards Warren—either way we'd wind up going in circles. Finally, we got the beast going in the proper direction.

"It's working," I yelled excitedly.

"Let's take her out a little further," Granddad Angus said.

BLAM!!!

It happened just as we were heading out into the deeper water.

Somebody was shooting at us with a shotgun that thought it was a gi-freaking-gantic cannon. Prehistoric moose hide gave way to a blast of buckshot, fired by some eager hunter crouching on the shoreline. I ducked and Dulsie screamed...or it might have been the other way around.

BLAM!!!

Another shotgun blast.

Things were happening fast, but not fast enough for my liking.

"Full speed ahead," I called out, cranking on my pedal-propeller just as hard as I could manage. Warren matched me, most of the time, and the old dory monster took off slowly, wallowing through the water like a cement speedboat.

"Slow it down," Granddad Angus said. "This rig wasn't built for speed."

His warning came too late.

Warren leaned into his pedal-propeller and the dory monster tipped sideways. I slid off my bicycle seat and fell against Warren's shoulder. All at once the water of Muddy Lake slopped into the gut of the dory monster and began pulling us down.

"Bail the boat out," Warren said, frantically scooping water with the cup of his palm.

"Never mind bailing the boat," Granddad Angus shouted back. "Bail the water."

I tried not to panic.

I tried to think calm thoughts.

The lake wasn't that deep.

We weren't that far from shore.

But all I could think about was a pack of Cub Scouts and bubbles coming up and for a long, slow, frozen moment in time I thought I could hear the roar of a skidoo and the crackle-snap of hungry breaking ice.

"We're sinking!" Warren shouted.

The dory monster kept on tipping. I reached up and tried to find something to hang on to, but all I caught hold of was the skin of my purple glitter banana seat. The vinyl was slick with lake water and my grip wouldn't hold and I tipped sideways and slid out through the side of the sea monster. I hit the lake, opened my mouth to yell, and swallowed a horking lungful of dirty lake water.

The last thing I heard was Dulsie screaming like a scalded banshee. I don't know why she screamed. She was in the boat, the same as everyone else. I was the one who had fallen in and was most likely about to drown to death.

And then I was under.

Chapter 17

SEA SERPENT: SIGHTED, SHOT, AND SINKING

Things happen fast when you don't want them to.

I was in the water, kicking hard. I might have been kicking upwards or I might have been kicking down towards the bottom. It was hard to tell. The lake water was cold and dark. I think I saw a foot flash by my head. It might have belonged to Granddad Angus or Warren or Dulsie. I tried not to swallow but the water kept pushing past my lips. I could taste it. I did my best not to choke. I tried to stay calm. That's what you're supposed to do, isn't it?

Don't panic, I told myself.

Try and drown calmly.

I sank a little deeper, in spite of my kicking.

Just how deep was this lake, anyway?

From down here in the deep darkness I could see the faces of the ghosts of those missing Cub Scouts staring up at me, looming like soft white jellyfish. The closest ghost reached out a glowing hand and touched my arm. Then he said something to me. Not in words, not the kind that you speak. He said something to me in the same way that a cool breeze will talk to you on a hot August after-noon and whisper of school and snowplows and leaves falling away.

You can stay here with us, is what his feelings said to me.

I'm not ready to stay just yet, is what I felt back—and then a warm, calm kind of glow seeped into my bones. For a moment I was absolutely certain that for some unfathomable reason I had stopped sinking.

I smiled a little and swallowed and started to choke and then something grabbed hold of my neck. I felt myself being dragged upwards. "Whaaaawwhackhwahakchwahak."

I emerged from the water, hacking and coughing and glad to be able to breathe. Warren held the back of my neck tight enough to cut off my circulation. I'd always imagined if I found myself in a life-or-death situation it would be Granddad Angus who'd save me.

Never in my wildest dreams had I imagined boring old Warren Boudreau would dive into a bottomless lake and save my life. I hacked and coughed a bit more to hide my surprise.

"You can swim, can't you?" Warren asked.

I nodded, only half hearing him. I kept thinking about those ghostly Cub Scouts I had seen. I kept looking back behind me, but there was nothing but lake water and a whole lot of cold. All I could see were the moonbeams shining fat and white spotlight haloes over the deep, silent waters of Muddy Lake.

"Lean on Fogopogo and keep kicking towards open water," he told me. "We need to put some distance between us and that shot-gun before we try and clamber back under the moose hide and into the dory."

I nodded weakly and hung on to the side of the dory monster, kicking with the strength of a half-frozen pollywog. Warren was in the water, kicking right along with me. All the while Granddad Angus kept asking me if I was okay and I kept nodding back, like he could hear my head bobbing up and down.

"He's fine, Angus," Warren sputtered. "And we're almost there."

We kicked out into the lake. The shotgun blasted a few more times, but it sounded as if whoever was shooting was aiming in all the wrong directions. I clambered into the dory like I was three-parts sea monkey and helped Warren back under the cover of moose hide and crow feathers. Granddad Angus hugged me and held me like he was still afraid I was going to drift away.

"That was fun," Warren said, grinning as if he'd somehow caught Granddad Angus's knock-knock-joke grin. "Let's do it again."

"Dad!" Dulsie exclaimed in disbelief.

"We need more weight in the dory," Granddad Angus suggested, finally letting me go. "Dories sail best if they're loaded to the gunnels with a cargo of dead fish."

I kept thinking about how we had very nearly become a cargo of dead fish only I didn't say anything because I could tell that Granddad Angus had been pretty scared for me.

Not that I'd needed any help being scared.

"Head for the river," Granddad Angus went on. "Just in case whoever did all that shooting decides to straighten out his aim."

I kept looking behind me back towards the cold swallow of that dark old lake. A part of me wondered what it would have been like to just settle down to the bottom. A bigger part of me was Christmas-morning happy that I hadn't actually drowned.

The lake wasn't telling me anything. If there was a story hidden down there it sure wasn't doing much talking right now.

Except, just for an instant, I thought I saw the face of a boy poking up out of the water, grinning at me. I waved. The boy held his fingers up in the Cub Scout salute and waved back.

"What are you waving at, Roland?" Warren wanted to know.

He looked back when he asked me and I don't believe he saw what I did. I might have just imagined the whole thing. Nearly drowning could surely bring on hallucinations, but another part of me, hidden deeper inside, told me that maybe what I was looking at was a little more than real.

"Nothing," I said. "I'm just waving at nothing."

"We'd better get this into the shore and pick up some ballast before we try to take it any further," Granddad Angus said.

We needed to get the oars out to steer the monster towards the river bank. Once we got into shallow enough water, Granddad Angus handed me one of the oars.

"Lean on that and push down hard and forward," he told me. "Push against the stone of the riverbed and get us in close enough to wade ashore."

I caught hold of the oar and leaned into it.

Just for a moment I could feel the current of the river and the hard of the stone throbbing through the long grain of the oar. I could feel the ocean's tug further down the river and the wind blowing through the trees that leaned and nodded and bowed to the river. I could feel the seagulls soaring and I could count the waves that rolled into Deeper Harbour and somehow or other, amongst all the deep, strong feelings that rolled through the veins of my body for that half a second, I could feel Granddad Angus grinning at me.

Dulsie and me and Warren waded ashore and loaded some good river stone into the belly of Fogopogo to keep him weighted safely in the water. Granddad Angus held the monster while we loaded. We pushed off once again.

We tested the dory in the shallow water, rocking and jumping to make sure we weren't going to take on any more water. I leaned on Warren and we pedal-paddled as hard as we could. Even with Dulsie leaning in the same direction, the monster safely held its course without tipping.

I looked forward as we moved down the river, aiming our sea beast towards the open mouth of the Drain and out towards the ocean.

Chapter 18

DOWN THE DRAIN

Riding down the winding stream of the Drain felt a little like cruising down the very large and very wet throat of a sea monster. I wasn't sure if we were being swallowed or fur-ball-hacked back up. That quiet little river had a stronger current than I had ever imagined. The current pushed and tugged on Fogopogo like the big old dory monster was nothing but a crumple of soggy toilet paper.

It got worse as we left the mouth of the Drain and began moving into the open sea. The waves fought us at first, as if the ocean was trying to slap us uppity dry-landers back to shore. The water didn't look rough in the growing dawn light, but there were currents moving deep down below the surface that were talking to the dory in a way we couldn't ignore.

"Work those grinders for me while I row now," Granddad Angus called out to me. He slid his backup pair of oars into the oarlocks and started rowing, while Warren steered with the rudder. "Keep her hard a'port, Warren."

"Right, Angus," Warren replied.

"I thought port was to the left," I joked.

I told the joke because it was the only way I could unclench my teeth and my jaw was beginning to hurt. I had never been out to sea in a dory before now, and it scared me a little. That was something that had changed in Deeper Harbour since Dad was a boy. Back then children grew up close to the water and learned the ways of the sea at a very early age. Granddad Angus had Dad out in a dory on his tenth birthday.

The waves weren't that rough, but the dory monster heaved and rolled just the same and my stomach heaved and rolled along with it. I was beginning to have second thoughts about that plate of fried eggs I had eaten before leaving. Dulsie didn't look too good either. The green in her face wasn't all face paint, as near as I could tell.

"You're feeling a little seasick, are you?" Granddad Angus called out.

"I feel like I'm about to heave my toes up through my eye teeth," I told him. "If this is seasick, I'm seasick with a capital C. We ought to land this dory."

I wasn't joking. At this point in the game I was ready to give up and go home and pack my bags for Ottawa. I told Granddad Angus just that.

"The human spirit is like a boat on a wave," Granddad Angus said. "The wave will toss you up and roll you down and the only thing you can do is ride out the trough and pray for the crest. As bad as you feel now I guarantee you will feel ten times better tomorrow."

I wasn't so sure about that.

"This isn't a dory anymore," Granddad Angus went on. "It's a story and a legend just waiting to be born. We've built a sea monster and we're in this just as deep as we can get. There's no backing out now."

That's the part that bothered me. The whole "deep" business. I mean, it wasn't as if we were going to dog-paddle our way out of the Atlantic Ocean if this sea monster went and sank on us.

I was scared. There was no other word for it.

Pure chicken-cluck scared.

"What if we capsize again?"

"We're not going to capsize," Granddad Angus assured me. "That only happened because we panicked."

I still wasn't convinced.

This was Granddad Angus, a man who had made a lifetime out of doing stupid things. Who in their right mind would listen to him?

"This is stupid, stupid, stupid," I said for about the four thousandth time.

"Of course it's stupid," Warren said. "It's supposed to be stupid. Anyone who has never done anything stupid in their life has never tried anything new."

All three of us looked at Warren in total surprise. We had come to expect words of caution and common sense from Warren and here he was sounding almost like some sort of a daredevil.

"Albert Einstein said it before I did," Warren explained, with a sheepish shrug. "I have a stamp with him on it."

"My dad used to say something like that to me," Granddad Angus said. "'If you've never been lost, you've never really rowed far enough away from the shore.'"

Which made even less sense to me.

"This is stupid with a capital stupid, squared to an unlimited infinity of stupid," I said. "I want to go home."

"Do you mean Deeper Harbour or Ottawa?" Granddad Angus asked.

I thought about that.

He had a point.

"We're almost there, aren't we?" I said.

"The harbour is just ahead," Granddad Angus said. "Just around that big stony point."

When we rounded the point I could see the harbour, but from a perspective I'd never had before. Not this early in the morning. Not all new and all fresh like it was. It was almost as if I had somehow grown myself a whole new set of eyes.

I'd grown up here and I'd learned to skip a stone and throw a ball and ride a bike all within a stone's throw of this sleepy little coastal town. But looking at it this morning, from the belly of a homemade sea monster, everything looked strangely different. The harbour was peaceful and welcoming and I could see all the wonderful details that a tourist might notice.

Sure, there was no McDonald's.

Sure, there was no movie theatre.

Sure, there weren't any tourist attractions.

The fog curled and clotted about buildings that leaned like old, tired men. The paint was peeling and the only signs of life were a few early fishermen who looked up and probably blinked a few times while trying to decide if a sea monster was worth catching or throwing back. Even the seagulls looked more than a little bored with the way the tide of time seemed to stand so still around this sleepy little harbour town.

But there was something quiet and precious and forever in the way that our little town clung there like a barnacle upon a wave-worn rock. There was something that caught in my throat like a swallow of surprise birthday party.

Then one of the fishermen stood up and pointed.

Granddad Angus woofed through his birchbark moose call.

A fishing boat blew its sounding horn, long and low and clear.

Maybe that fishing boat was saying hello. Maybe that fishing boat was warning us to stay away from its fishing grounds. Maybe that old boat was just clearing something from its throat.

But it was the figure standing alone on the wharf that caught my attention.

A figure that stood there as if whoever it was had been standing there all morning just waiting for us to pedal-paddle into the harbour.

I couldn't see him clearly enough to be certain, but I could feel him deep in my heart. I was sure it was my dad, standing there watching me sail in the belly of a moose-hide and crow-feather sea monster.

He was holding something in his hand, high above his head.

"That person's got a cell phone," Dulsie said with more than a little certainty. "I'm pretty sure whoever that is, they're making a Fogopogo video."

"Everybody say cheese," Granddad Angus said.

And underneath the moose hide and the chicken wire and the crow feathers, we all smiled.

Whoever it was, standing on the wharf, waved before turning away.

By the end of the day we had our own YouTube video.

It was a blurry, out-of-focus, shaky-handed video that showed something that might have been a sea monster or might have been a giant floating whale booger. It showed just enough to give the impression that the video was showing something very out of the ordinary.

We had actual video coverage.

The word was getting out.

Chapter 19

HOT PURSUIT

We had to wait three more days for another foggy morning.

By now nearly everyone in the town had seen the video of Fogopogo. Nora hooked up a wall-sized television in her diner so that everyone could watch it. Opinions were divided about just whether the blurry image on the video was a sea monster or not.

While we waited for the fog to roll in, we hid Fogopogo in the belly of a tidal cove that was sheltered by a thicket of pine trees. It was a perfect hiding spot that allowed us to work at keeping the sea monster patched up and running without being discovered by any curious townsfolk.

We set off on our next excursion before the sun rose, sliding out carefully into the ocean water and aiming ourselves towards that big old cape of a rock that hooked out around the harbour like a fat man's arm around a plate full of beans. I was still afraid of tipping over, but the ballast we had set in the belly of the dory monster seemed to keep it at an even keel.

So far, so good.

The fishermen were out again. This time they didn't even seem to notice us. They were far too busy tending to their lines and cleaning their boats and making certain that everything was ready for the day. That was just how fishermen were, no matter what time of day it was. Everything revolved around the boat that they staked their lives on and the prospect of their next catch. A little thing like a sea monster wasn't going to upset their daily routine.

This time I could see the purple minivan parked just beside Warren's boat shed.

That minivan was more important than the fishermen. The monster-hunters were bound to help spread the word even further.

I could see a few more people out there as well. It looked as if every customer in Nora's Diner had cleared out from the early breakfast special and lined up in front of the restaurant, gawking out into the harbour.

Which was about when one of the fishing boats burped and chuttered to life and started heading straight towards us. It might have been the same boat that had blown its horn at us on our first trip out. We were too far away to tell, and even though we knew all those fishermen by name, through the fog all their boats looked the same.

About the only thing that we could be certain of was that he was definitely determined to give us chase.

"Turn it hard, Roland," Granddad Angus ordered. "Warren, you ease off."

Warren eased up on his pedal-paddling and I turned the pedal as hard as I could. The monster swung around slowly.

"Pedal harder," Dulsie said.

All the while, the fishing boat kept getting closer. I expected that the captain was trying to figure just how much per pound a full-grown sea monster was going to net him, but I was determined not to let him catch us.

Still, a pedal-paddling dory monster isn't much of a match for a six-hundred-horsepower engine. We really didn't stand much of a chance until Granddad Angus stepped into action. He woofed menacingly into the moose call.

I couldn't be certain, but I believe the fishing boat slowed down a little after that woof. Meanwhile, Warren and I kept on working the pedal-paddles, and Dulsie slipped the backup oars into their locks and began to row just as hard as she could. It helped a bit, but the boat kept getting closer.

"Steer for the shallows," Granddad Angus said. "Once we put those rocks behind us that fishing boat is bound to head for easier waters."

Granddad Angus had calculated correctly.

Or else the fishing boat captain had reconsidered running his boat up against a sea monster.

"Next time bring a bigger boat!" Dulsie called out playfully, once we were far enough around the harbour mouth to be out of sight.

I was still scared. Nearly being caught didn't help my worry at all.

"What if they had caught us?" I asked.

"They probably would have thrown us back," Warren said. "Your grandfather would have made for some pretty tough cleaning."

Warren's joke didn't stop me from worrying. What if next time they sent out the Coast Guard? What if next time they had a navy destroyer waiting for us? What if we were shelled with cannon fire or depth charges?

Suddenly, this whole idea didn't seem half as fun.

"This is Deeper Harbour," Granddad Angus told me after I confided my fear. "The only depth charges we need to worry about are the ones that follow the church's baked-bean and brown-bread supper."

I wasn't so sure about that.

"We could try taking Fogopogo out at night," Warren suggested. "We'd catch two fish with one hook that way. We'd be a whole lot more concealed and we wouldn't have to worry about waiting for the fog to roll in."

That made sense to me but Granddad Angus thought differently.

"The first three letters in Fogopogo tells it all, as far as I'm concerned. Fog is a part of the mystery of the story," he said. "Besides, I need my sleep."

He was being funny but I knew that he was right. Keeping to foggy mornings meant that sooner or later people would clue in and start watching the harbour every morning a little fog rolled in. It made it easier to guarantee a built-in audience.

Just so long as the four of us didn't get caught.

Chapter 20

FOGOPOGO MAKES THE NEWS

So far, the whole plan was working.

Everything was happening just exactly as I'd dreamed it would. Every time we took Fogopogo out into the harbour the story grew a little more. People began to spread rumours of their own. Even the people who hadn't seen Fogopogo yet had begun to talk about the monster as if they'd actually seen it firsthand.

"Fogopogo is bigger than Loch Ness."

"Fogopogo is bigger than Bigfoot."

"Fogopogo is bigger than King Kong standing on top of Godzilla's grass-green eyebrows."

When we didn't have fog, we still did our best to kept the pot stirred up.

Granddad Angus made a recording of his best moose call, and I used my computer to make the noise sound like an entire flotilla of sea monsters. Dulsie started hiding in the woods around the town, playing Fogopogo's roar through Dad's electronic bullhorn, which he thought was still locked in the supply closet at the police station.

"If we can keep people on their toes and guessing," Granddad Angus said, "we can keep Fogopogo alive between sightings."

Warren was more than a little worried about somebody taking a shot in the general direction of Dulsie.

"One shotgun blast in a lifetime is plenty for me," Warren said.

I guess I couldn't really blame Warren for worrying like he did. I suppose that after having Dulsie's mother die, Warren was bound to be worried about losing his daughter too.

Dulsie thought the whole thing was a great big adventure. She began a series of today tattoos in the pattern of killer commando camouflage, only instead of the traditional green, yellow, and brown, Dulsie used nearly every colour imaginable and a few that hadn't even been thought up yet.

"Who do you think you are?" Warren asked her. "Rambo?"

"She looks more like a rainbow to me," Granddad Angus said.

Rainbow or Rambo, we were all working hard to spread the word about Fogopogo.

After our third sailing, Fogopogo and Deeper Harbour were mentioned in most of the larger newspapers in the country. Talk-show hosts and newscasters were arguing back and forth about whether the sea monster was real or a hoax.

Molly decided that the news articles should be preserved in the town archives, which, so far, consisted of a closet full of shoeboxes crammed full of clippings and old photos. She gave Fogopogo his very own shoebox and photocopied every article about him and posted it up on a bulletin board that Warren nailed to the side of his boat shed for just that purpose.

Every morning that I wasn't out in the monster I checked on the latest news clippings.

SEA MONSTER SPOTTED OUTSIDE OF SLEEPY FISHING VILLAGE

That paper had a fuzzy picture of Fogopogo in it that showed just enough monster to get people to read the story.

IS FOGOPOGO REAL?

That story was written by someone who wanted very badly to prove that there are no sea monsters, and he compared Fogopogo to a UFO. The writer had decided that the entire phenomenon was nothing more than a case of shared delusions.

Personally, I think he just wanted to use the word "phenomenon."

My favourite article had to be the clipping from a British para-normal magazine with a headline that read "FOGOPOGO—FIEND OF THE ATLANTIC." It described Fogopogo as blood-curdling and dangerous.

Wow.

I felt like a mad scientist.

I had helped build a monster.

A fiend.

Cool.

Chapter 21

SITTING STILL AND SETTING WORLD SPEED RECORDS

"The whole town is out there," I said.

We were into our third week of taking Fogopogo out and I don't believe I had ever seen so much of Deeper Harbour gathered together at any one time. They were all there, by the dozens and hundreds. I could see the purple minivan and the glint of a telescope and I hoped that the bit of morning mist we'd counted on was enough to disguise the fact we were but a moose-hide-clad dory.

Granddad Angus woofed out the grandfather of all turnip farts, through the birchbark moose call. It sounded horrible from inside the moose hide, but roaring and echoing through the mist and the waves, it must have sounded pretty impressive. I heard folks cheering and one woman screamed, the way you might scream at a tightrope act in the circus.

I could see the people on shore clearly now. They were clustered around the wharf and I could see them pointing. We were far enough out that none of the onlookers could get a clear look at us and the morning mist made things even eerier.

Or at least I hoped so.

Again, I saw the glint of a telescope or maybe binoculars. A part of me wanted to crouch down, even though I knew that the sea monster safely hid anybody in the dory.

I peeked through my peephole and I could see the big stretch of grey rock that hooked out around the harbour.

"Keep working those grinders," Granddad Angus warned me.

"I'm turning them as hard as I can," I told him. "I just don't seem to be getting anywhere."

"Seems that way, doesn't it?" Granddad Angus said.

"What do you mean, 'seems that way'?" I asked. "It is that way. This is really hard."

Granddad Angus just shook his head.

"What's that supposed to mean?" I asked.

"At any given time the Earth is rotating upon its axis at nearly 1,700 kilometres an hour," Warren said. "At the same time, the planet is orbiting around the sun at the speed of 108,000 kilometres per hour."

I blinked.

Warren had definitely out-stranged himself.

"So what's that supposed to mean?" I asked.

"He means you're setting world speed records just sitting still," Dulsie explained.

Which still didn't make much sense to me.

"I don't get it," I said.

"What he means," Granddad Angus said, "is that it is impossible to sit still for very long, at least as long as you're sitting upon this planet. Life has a strong current that will pull you forward into ever deeper water no matter how hard you try to stay in one place."

"How'd you ever get to be so smart?" I said.

"Never try and debate astrophysics with a dory man," Granddad Angus said.

"Or a stamp collector," Warren added.

"Or a punk-goth-freakazoid," Dulsie chimed in.

"Is that a fact?" I asked.

"I said so, didn't I?" Granddad Angus asked.

I looked over at my Granddad Angus, sitting there in the belly of that homemade sea monster, his face lit up and mottled by the sunlight leaking through the shot-up moose hide. He was smiling softly and just for that moment I had the feeling that my entire life was orbiting gently about that smile.

"It's really going to work, isn't it?" I said.

"Did you ever think it wouldn't?" Granddad Angus answered.

Chapter 22

DEEPER HARBOUR AVALANCHE

Have you ever built a snowman? Do you know how it is when you start rolling it from a little snowball up into a great big snow-boulder? Do you know that part when it gets so heavy that you really have to work each step and lean hard and it just keeps getting heavier and you just keep rolling because some little voice inside you keeps whispering, *Just a little bigger*?

We were way past that snowball-rolling point.

We were into avalanche and abominable snowman country.

Now everyone was really paying attention to Deeper Harbour. Two Maritime news shows came to town and the monster-hunters were interviewed by three different radio stations. A bunch of re-porters tried to interview Dad, but they stopped calling after he used a few words I never thought I'd hear being uttered over the police station telephone.

And we had received our first tour bus.

It brought twelve tourists, all told, who wandered through the streets and ate at Nora's Diner. Postcards were bought and pictures taken before they funnelled back onto the bus and made their way out of town.

"This sea monster is great for business," I heard my mom say.

Yes!

If Mom thinks there's hope for Deeper Harbour then maybe she won't be so quick to uproot us.

Nora had to bring in a second cook for the diner. She started to sell Fogopogo dogs. She took foot-long wieners, dipped them in homemade cornbread batter, and deep-fried them. She served them up with ketchup, mustard, or a green chili salsa that she claimed was hot enough to peel paint.

Which it was.

Meanwhile, Molly revived the town newspaper, a three-page bulletin stapled together that she called the *Deeper Harbour Digest*, and sold it at the drugstore for fifty cents apiece. She announced that there would be a contest and a prize given to whomever managed to get a clear photo of Fogopogo.

Warren set up a souvenir shop in his boat shed. He started selling Fogopogo t-shirts and hats and stuffed sea monsters, all of which sold pretty well. He also made some homemade lemonade and sold it by the glass and scooped ice cream into cones, until Dad told him that he would need a permit to sell food. That put an end to the ice cream and lemonade business.

Dulsie had the best idea of all though.

She came up with the idea of a sea-serpent egg.

She asked Warren to drive to Yarmouth to buy a pickled ostrich egg from an ostrich farmer and then she painted the egg with food colouring.

Warren displayed the egg in a second-hand aquarium he bought at a yard sale along with a bag full of plastic dinosaurs that he had kept from when Dulsie was a little girl. I thought it was neat how

Dulsie had played with toy dinosaurs, but she swore that she had never seen them before in her life.

As a finishing touch Warren had Dulsie paint a sign that read, "FOGOPOGO EGG???"

"I put the three question marks on the sign so that it wouldn't exactly be a lie," Warren explained. "You see, I'm not really claiming that the egg is a sea monster egg. I'm just asking a question, is all."

I thought that Warren was drawing an awfully thin line to stand behind, but since I was the one who had first come up with the whole idea of making a sea monster, I certainly couldn't call him dishonest for trying to attract a little more attention. Besides, he was so excited to have finally found a way to make a little money from the old boat shed.

"He had started selling my grandpa's old boat-building tools as antiques," Dulsie explained. "We were that short of money."

I was just glad to have accidentally done something that helped Dulsie.

I still wasn't ready to call her my girlfriend, mind you.

For now I was happy enough just calling her my friend.

Dad wasn't nearly as excited about all the new people that the Fogopogo sightings had brought to town. He'd had to start issuing speeding tickets and had arrested a couple of drunk drivers.

"If this keeps up I might actually have to hire a whole police force," he said.

He especially wasn't happy with the litter from all those people, and I couldn't blame him. There were coffee cups and hamburger wrappers and doughnut bags drifting amongst the rocks and salt grass of the harbour.

"I'd call this place a pigsty," Dad said. "Except that would mean I'd have to apologize to pigs all over the world."

Personally, I thought that Dad was just being a bit too much of a party-pooper. Couldn't he see how good all this was for our little town?

I wanted to try and explain to him how this whole scheme was going to bring tourism back to Deeper Harbour. That way Mom wouldn't have to leave and take me to Ottawa and I could stay here with him.

And we could all live happily ever after.

Everybody else I talked to seemed awfully excited about all of the business that Fogopogo was bringing to Deeper Harbour. It seemed like the whole town wanted a piece of our little sea monster.

So it was only a matter of time before somebody got the bright idea to hold a Fogopogo Festival.

PART IV

THE FRIDAY FOGOPOGO FESTIVAL FREAK-O-RAMA

Chapter 23

THE CHICKENS WIN AGAIN

Maritimers are always ready for a party.

They will declare a festival over nearly anything you can imagine.

There's an annual pumpkin regatta Windsor, Nova Scotia, where people paddle pumpkin-boats across Lake Pezaquid, and in Wolfville, they stage a rubber duck race every spring. Every summer, there is a bathtub race in Marion Bridge, Nova Scotia. In New Brunswick, there's even a festival for fiddleheads, those chewy little ferns that Granddad Angus swears are as tasty as all get out.

So why not have a Fogopogo Festival?

"It's perfect," I said. "The town council has finally got it right. Now there is no way on earth that Mom can say Deeper Harbour is dying."

The four of us stood there in Warren's boat shed—Granddad Angus, Warren, Dulsie, and I.

"It's time we called an end to this," Granddad Angus said. "It is getting way too risky."

"What do you think is going to happen?" Warren asked. "Do you figure they're going to send in the Canadian Navy?"

"We haven't finished what we started," I pointed out.

"Yeah," Dulsie agreed. "There's still a lot more that needs doing."

Granddad Angus shook his head like a tired old bull.

"We're in the papers," he said. "And we're on the national news. Tourists are hearing about us. Now we've got this Fogopogo Festival happening. What else do we need to do?"

We all started arguing at once but Granddad Angus wasn't hearing any of it.

"It's too risky," Granddad Angus said. "I never really dreamed it would go as far as it has."

I couldn't believe what I was hearing.

Here, all along I had been scared and worried and looking towards my granddad to keep my courage afloat. This was absolutely the first time that Granddad Angus had shown the least bit of doubt.

"But it's perfect," I repeated. "Everybody will be there. They'll all have cameras, and there will be reporters and film crews, and booths selling popcorn and candy and balloons."

"Cutting into my business, they will be," Warren said with a worried look.

"Warren," I said. "Your business is t-shirts and a painted ostrich egg. How badly do you think that's going to be hurt by someone selling sea monster balloons?"

"It's too risky," Granddad Angus repeated. "All of those people. Somebody is bound to notice that their sea monster is nothing but a couple of old fogeys and a pair of young kids in a tarted-up dory."

"Who are you calling a fogey?" Warren wanted to know.

"If the shoe fits…," Granddad Angus began.

Only I wasn't about to let the subject get changed.

"This is our big chance," I argued. "If Fogopogo turns up for the Fogopogo Festival, we'll have tourists in town year-round, hoping for a sea serpent sighting."

"It's too risky," Granddad Angus repeated.

"Buck, buck, buckaw," Dulsie began.

All three of us turned to see Dulsie Jane Boudreau doing her world-famous chicken dance. I joined right in immediately, jamming my fists up under my armpits and flapping my elbows like there was no tomorrow.

"Buck, buck, buckaw," I said.

It was wearing on him. I could tell. Not even Granddad Angus could resist the power of a well-timed double-dog dare.

"All right," he said. "All right. You have talked me into it."

He fixed a hard stare in Warren's direction.

"Buck, buck, buck?" Warren asked.

"Go buck yourself," Granddad Angus said. "Fogopogo is going to ride again. But this is the very last time."

Granddad Angus was almost right.

Chapter 24

DOWN-HOME COOKING

Later that day Dad sizzled up some garlic sausage and a chopped onion and some apple slices in the fry pan. Then he dumped two tins of beans on top of that, drizzled in a little maple syrup, and buttered a couple of slices of bread that looked suspiciously as if they might have been made out of rocks, twigs, and seeds.

"High fibre he-man beans," Dad said. "I bet you didn't know your dad was a gourmet chef."

"Since when do you know how to cook?" I asked.

He grinned and winked.

For just an instant I felt this weird sort of Stephen King moment, as if I was staring at Granddad Angus wearing Dad's face, cooking like Mom.

"It might be there are a lot of things you don't know about your dad."

The food tasted good. I was hungry from a morning of pedal-paddling. We had left the dory monster in the inlet, covered with deadfall and pine boughs. As far as we could tell, it was nearly invisible. Of course, Dad didn't know anything of that. At least I was pretty certain he didn't know.

You never can tell with Dad, though.

He can surprise you.

"It's good to see you spending so much time with your grand-father," Dad said.

He's not just my grandfather was what I wanted to say.

Only I just nodded.

"I even kind of envy you getting the chance to leave Deeper Harbour."

What?

Now where did that come from?

Just like that, I lost it completely.

I threw my fork down. It did a little hop-skiddle in the beans, spattering bean sauce on Dad's paper tablecloth.

"Envy me? I don't want to go. I hate Ottawa. And I hate my mother. All I want to do is to stay here with you and Granddad Angus."

I stared up at him as if I had laser vision and could burn a hole through his skull deep enough to penetrate whatever common sense he had buried beneath the layers of grilled cheese sand-wiches and he-man beans. I knew he would slap me. I had seen all the movies where the kid badmouths his mother and the dad slaps the kid and tells him that he must never talk bad about his mother.

Only Dad didn't slap me.

He just sat there staring at me.

Not saying a word.

I think he must have had some sort of an evil shrinking ray hidden in his silence because by the time he was done not talking I felt a little less than two inches tall.

"So what were you up to all day today?" he finally asked.

I was in the belly of a dory monster named Fogopogo, was what

I wanted to tell him. *I was sitting in a moose hide with your father*, was what I wanted to say.

"Nothing," was all I said.

"So did you see the sea monster this morning?" he asked.

"Sure," I said. "Didn't everybody?"

"Funny," he said. "But I was down at the wharf and I didn't see you anywhere."

I shrugged and swallowed. It was hard to lie to my dad but I had to.

"It was a big crowd, wasn't it?" I said.

Dad nodded. I wasn't so sure what a police chief would think about a crowd like that, especially since Dad had been complaining about the mess the tourists were making of the town. I was afraid that he might feel that so many people gathered so close to the water was a public hazard or something.

Only he surprised me.

"You know what?" he said. "I can't remember ever seeing so many people in our town so excited over any one thing."

"Not even on bingo night?" I asked.

"Not even bingo night," Dad answered. "Whatever this sea monster is, I believe it's doing a pretty good thing for Deeper Harbour."

And then he looked right at me and winked one more time.

"Do you know what I heard?" he asked.

And then he told me who was coming to Deeper Harbour.

And it wasn't David Suzuki.

Chapter 25

CLOTHESLINE-CABER
EVOLUTION

People will surprise you any chance they get.

It turned out that Warren already knew who was coming to Deeper Harbour. He'd known for quite a while. He told us all about it while we carried Molly's clothesline pole back to her backyard.

Or at least we were carrying what used to be Molly's clothesline pole. Granddad Angus had changed it considerably. That was just what Granddad Angus did, I guess. He laid his hands on things and they changed. It had been a pine tree that had become a clothesline pole and then Granddad Angus had changed that pole into a caber.

And then he'd changed it one more time.

He'd changed it in the dark of Warren's boat shed, working alone on it with a mallet and gouge and chisel whenever we weren't out in the dory monster, turning that clothesline-pole caber into something else.

Something beautiful.

Granddad Angus had carved the top of Molly Winter's clothesline-pole caber into a sea serpent.

"I got the idea from Dulsie's today tattoos," Granddad Angus said. "I wanted to make something out of this old caber before we gave it back to Molly and set it up for her as a clothesline pole again."

The top of the caber was the sea serpent's head and the rest of its body wound down around the body of the clothesline pole, with its tail curled neatly around the base. It was painted and thickly covered with at least three coats of marine varnish.

"I had Dulsie paint in the details and I glued two chips of amethyst where the eyes are supposed to go."

I stared at it, thinking to myself how amazing it was that this old Jack pine had been cut down and used as a clothesline pole until Granddad Angus turned it into a caber and then threw it through a dory and now both dory and clothesline pole had grown up into sea monsters.

Dulsie, Warren, Granddad Angus, and I carried the pole down to Molly's house and nearly half the town followed us. Some of them even helped carry the sea serpent clothesline pole. While we were carrying it I told Granddad Angus and Dulsie and Warren about who was coming to town.

Which was when Warren told us that he'd already known who was coming to town.

Like I said, people will surprise you.

"The prime minister of Canada himself is coming to Deeper Harbour," Warren confirmed, "for the town's annual Fogopogo Festival."

It struck me a little funny how something that had just been invented could suddenly be described as annual. I guess that it was something like a dream, painted with the hope that a festival and a town could outlast a new highway.

"I bet he read my letter," Warren went on. He was about the

most excited I'd ever seen him. "He wants to meet with me, I know it. I bet you he's hoping to get a good look at Fogopogo."

Granddad Angus snorted.

"My guess is he reads the newspaper," he said. "I expect the man knows a photo opportunity when he sees it."

"No," Warren said. "He's coming because he got my letter. I just know he is."

Granddad Angus still wasn't convinced.

"It must be an election year," Granddad Angus said. "I wonder if he thinks that sea monsters can vote."

"Say what you want, Angus," Warren argued. "When he gets here, I expect him to see this sea monster. And I intend to be there with him when he sees it."

"Well, how will we move that rig without you to help?" asked Granddad Angus, lowering his voice.

"You'll just have to figure out a way," Warren replied. "I need to make as much profit out of this as I can."

"Do you figure he's going to give you money?" Dulsie asked.

"They're called grants, girl. Prime ministers give them out all the time."

I wasn't so sure about Warren's logic, but there was no reasoning with the man. He had his heart set on getting next to the prime minister and pumping his arm like a pump handle.

"Since when did you get so greedy?" Granddad Angus asked.

"I've got expenses to deal with," Warren said. "Up until now the only way I've made any money out of that boat shed has been selling some of my dad's tools to an antique dealer."

"Why don't you just sell the shed and be done with it?" Dulsie asked.

"I've got plans for that shed," Warren said.

"Plans?" Granddad Angus said with a snort of derision. "You figuring on expanding your ostrich egg exhibit?"

"I've got plans," Warren repeated.

And that's all he would tell us.

Then we got to Molly's place and found out the truth of it.

Chapter 26

A STORY WITHOUT WORDS

Molly was surprised when over half of the town showed up at her door carrying a Jack-pine-sea-monster-caber-clothesline-pole. She bustled around and tried her best to make pancakes, but she was saved by Nora, who showed up with a couple of bushel baskets of deep-fried grilled cheese sandwiches.

It was really something to see.

I was a little surprised that people could find the time to go to Molly's, since everyone was so busy with their Fogopogo Festival preparations. The truth was, nearly everybody in town had been busy stringing streamers and repainting their houses and getting all of Deeper Harbour spruced up for the big day ahead.

The drugstore had a sea monster mural painted on its front window.

The town florist had a big sale on snapdragons.

The fishermen were decorating the fishing boats. They had built themselves a makeshift Chinese New Year's dancing dragon out of long, flowing sailcloth that they duct taped to a dozen dory oars. They practised dancing with that dragon every day.

The preparations were both awesome and inspiring, but everybody still managed to find the time to come down and take part in the restoration of Molly's pole. I guess that's how a town works. People help people any chance they get.

People chipped in and did their part as we dug a new hole and poured the cement and raised up the sea monster, while others helped to raise the section of Molly's fence that Granddad and I had trampled. We made sure that between the fence and a nearby tree it was almost impossible to see the sea serpent without actually coming into the yard.

"Me and Angus figure you'll be able to charge admission to come look at the sea monster," Warren explained. "If you get enough tourists, that'll make you some money to buy new books for the library."

Molly just shook her head sadly.

"There isn't going to be a library," she said. "The school is closing down. I don't think even the tourists coming back will stop that from happening."

Warren shrugged.

"I knew that already," he said. "And I've been trying to doing something about it."

We all stood there looking at him and waiting.

"I've been buying up lumber and building bookshelves in the back end of the boat shed," he told her. "It will take a while yet, but I believe there will be a brand new Deeper Harbour library ready for you by the fall."

So that was what Warren had needed the money for. And that was what he planned on doing with the shed. And that's what he hoped to get a grant for.

I felt a little embarrassed that Granddad Angus and I had given Warren such a very hard time when he had said he couldn't help us run Fogopogo anymore.

A lot of people said they would help Warren with the building supplies and insulation and wiring and they all sounded like they meant what they said. I looked at old boring Warren and wondered just where he had found the time to dream this up.

I guess people can surprise you if you let them.

Molly stood there and looked like she was going to cry.

Then she stepped over to Warren like a tidal wave rolling in on a dory, swooped him up in her arms and hugged him hard and kissed him even harder and, wonder upon wonders, Warren kissed back.

Dulsie looked at the two of them.

I could see anger and happiness arm wrestling in the shadows of her heart.

There was a story being told here, right before my eyes. There were no words involved and I did not know all of the details. I did not know all of the facts. I just knew that whatever this story was and however long it had been going on, it was the truest and deepest kind of story there is.

Finally, Dulsie stepped over and hugged the two of them. The whole town kept on cheering for the sea monster clothesline pole and Warren and Molly and the new library, while me and Granddad Angus grinned over what had just gone on.

Everyone was so happy.

Too bad things couldn't have stayed that way.

Chapter 27

GROUNDED WITHOUT GROUNDS

A day later, Mom was laying down the law again.

And all I could do was listen to her talk.

"This is an opportunity that you will not pass up," Mom said. "It's the prime minister of Canada, Roland."

"Can't we just wait to see him in Ottawa?" I asked.

"You don't just knock on the door at 24 Sussex Drive," Mom answered. "It just isn't that easy."

I figured if Mom knew the prime minister's home address she was probably on speaking terms with the man already. I wanted to tell her how Warren had gotten in touch with the prime minister just by sending him a common through-the-mail, Bigfoot-stamped letter, but then she would have asked me how I knew about that.

So I settled for, "Big deal."

"Don't argue with me, Roland," Mom said. "This is a chance to meet the prime minister of Canada, face to face."

"So what?" I said.

Which didn't help any more than "big deal" had.

"This isn't fair," I said. "You are grounding me without any grounds for evidence."

This approach had worked on a Law and Order episode three weeks ago, but I wasn't all that confident that it would work for me today.

"I have really had enough of arguing with you, Roland," Mom said. "This is a big opportunity and you will not miss it."

I was done arguing.

She had that mom-is-the-boss tone in her voice.

"Okay," I said.

Mom smiled.

"I bet this is really going to bring in the tourists," I said, hopefully.

Mom looked at me.

She knew what I was hinting at.

"You really do want to stay here, don't you?"

I nodded, hopefully. I'd seen all of the movies. I knew there was always a point after the kids had set up some crazy scheme that the parents would back down and see things properly.

Only this wasn't a movie.

Mom just shook her head. I could see she felt bad about it. I felt bad about feeling so mad at her. The two of us were stuck on opposite ends of emotion, not wanting to argue, but not able to agree.

"Do you know, except for when I went to university in Halifax, I have never been out of the town of Deeper Harbour?" Mom asked.

I hadn't known that.

She sighed, like she was missing something.

"Canada is such a big, wide country," she said. "There is so much of it to see. I'd like to see a little more of it before I need bifocals."

When she put it that way I felt bad about keeping her from fulfilling her dreams.

"Okay, Mom," I said. "You're right. This is a great opportunity."

I would go and meet the prime minister. I would stand there with Mom and Warren and the prime minister, waiting to see the Deeper Harbour sea monster.

I wondered if he would show up.

I wondered if we'd ever hear from David Suzuki.

But mostly I was wondering just how on earth was I going to tell Granddad Angus that I couldn't take the sea monster out with him tomorrow.

Chapter 28

MUTINY AND DESERTION

Have you ever known you had to say something, but not known how to say it?

"Hey" is usually where you begin.

I found Granddad Angus huddled under the moose hide, working on something close to the dory's bow.

"Hey," I said.

Granddad Angus almost hung himself stepping out from under the moose hide. As he stepped away, he dropped it down behind himself as if he were trying to hide something.

"What are you doing?" I asked.

"Dory stuff."

I nodded, like that made some kind of sense.

I wasn't really interested in whatever last-minute carpentry he was doing. I was still trying to figure out how to tell him that I wasn't going to be able to help him.

"It's great to see you," Granddad Angus said. He was clearly excited. "I've been working on a few ideas to make our monster go out with a big splash."

That sounded great to me—except I wasn't going to be any part of that great. I would be stuck on the shore with all the grown-ups, bored and alone.

So I told him what Mom had already told me.

"Mutiny and desertion," Granddad Angus said. "First Warren, then Dulsie, and now you. That's grounds for a flogging."

"Dulsie isn't going?" I said.

"She told me herself an hour ago," Granddad Angus said. "She says she has a top secret idea for making some money."

"She's got a job?"

"What part of top secret don't you understand?" Granddad Angus asked.

I still wasn't certain. I didn't like the idea of Granddad Angus taking the dory monster out by himself.

"I don't have to do what Mom and Dad tell me," I said. "I'm fourteen years old."

And then Granddad Angus surprised me.

"It's the prime minister of the country. You don't always have an opportunity like that," Granddad Angus said. "Your mother is right."

"Sure," I said. "Mom is always right. That's the problem. She's the worst thing that ever happened to Dad and me."

Granddad Angus threw his wooden mallet down. It bounced two or three times, nearly landing on my foot.

"Don't you ever say anything like that again," Granddad Angus told me.

I took a step back, just in case he wanted to throw the mallet again.

"Your mom is the best thing that ever happened to your father," Granddad Angus said. "I don't think I'll ever forgive him for letting her slip away."

"That's what happens though, isn't it?" I asked. "People get married and people get divorced. It happens all the time on television."

"Life isn't television," Granddad Angus said. "Life is a big wide ocean, which is why your eyes are dory-shaped, and not square."

"But it still happens."

"It didn't happen to me and my Marjorie," Granddad Angus said.

Marjorie was my grandmother. I didn't know much about her. When you're fourteen, people really don't tell you much. I had seen a picture or two and heard a story about how she'd loved to dance with Granddad Angus any chance she got. But that was all I really knew about her and I'd always meant to ask him to tell me more.

So I asked now.

"Tell me about her, Granddad," I asked.

Granddad Angus chewed a bit, as if there was something stuck in his teeth. I could tell he didn't want to talk, but I also knew I wasn't going to let him off the hook. I had a kind of funny feeling that he'd been wanting to tell me about her for a very long time, but just hadn't known how to begin.

"Start with 'hey,'" I suggested.

Finally, he cracked.

"Her name was Marjorie although everyone who knew her called her Madge. She was a patient woman," he began. "She waited patiently while I went out to sea. Sometimes I'd be gone for days and yet whenever I got home there'd be a hot meal and a pot of tea.

"She always knew," he went on. "I swear she could hear the bump of my dory hitting the wharf. And she never got tired of waiting. I'd always tell her that one of these days I'd be done with the water, but then off I'd go again."

"Why didn't you ever stay still?" I asked.

Granddad Angus shook his head ruefully.

"You might as well ask why the sea needs to be so deep," he said.

Then he looked away.

I could see that he was sinking.

I had to change the subject fast.

"Are you sure you're going to be okay out there?" I asked.

He just snorted scornfully in reply.

"What if there isn't any mist in the morning?" I asked.

"I've already thought of that," he assured me. "In fact, I've made a few changes to the old girl that I believe are going to knock you out of your sweat socks."

"Like what?" I asked.

"Wait and see."

I still wasn't so sure.

I had a very bad feeling about letting him take the monster out alone.

"What if they send out the navy?" I said. "What if there's a battleship out there, waiting to sink the sea monster?"

"Let them come," Granddad Angus said. "I'll be more than happy to show them how rough us old-time South Shore sailing men can be."

I had this sudden mental image of Granddad Angus blowing on his moose call and pedal-paddling like crazy up against a nuclear submarine.

"I can take it out alone," he told me. "Those pedal-paddles make for easy work. All I have to do is get out into deeper water and it'll be clear sailing."

I wasn't so certain about what Granddad Angus was telling me, but I wasn't in any position to argue with the man.

So I just smiled and nodded and grinned when he winked at me.

I wish I'd winked back.

Chapter 29

THE LONG BLACK LIMOUSINE OF FATE

Fridays are always fun, but the morning of the Fogopogo Festival looked to be one of the biggest and most important days in the history of Deeper Harbour.

The day started with a parade, the highlight of which was the dancing fishermen and their dragon. Wearing gumboots and waving the sailcloth dragon, the twelve fishermen made a fine spectacle of themselves.

Following the parade everyone gathered down at the wharf, just waiting to see the sea monster. The fogginess of the weather seemed like a guarantee that Fogopogo would make an appearance. At least that's what the festival planners were counting on.

I knew that Granddad Angus would make it happen. Fogopogo was going to be out there.

There was no way he would miss out on this.

There were people here from all over. I had never seen so many people crowded onto the wharf. I was a little worried the whole thing would tip into the ocean and float them away.

The prime minister showed up in a big black limousine and Mom and me and Warren and Molly piled in with him. I guess it had been Warren's letter that had done the trick.

The limousine was huge. In fact, I think they had to helicopter the limo into town because there was just no way I could imagine it making all the turns on the only road that led into Deeper Harbour.

Dulsie had refused to join us. She'd had her own idea and set up a face-painting booth in the shade of a big old birch tree just beside the boat shed, so she could take care of the sea serpent egg and t-shirts. She was making money painting the faces of the kids and some of the grown-ups who had forgotten that they weren't kids anymore. I know that might not sound like a big deal to anybody but I knew how happy Dulsie was getting a chance to use her face-painting skills for something that made sense to anyone else but herself.

As for me, I just couldn't stop smiling. This was exactly how things were supposed to turn out. It was like everything had come true the way I had seen it happen in my dreams.

It was fate.

Warren sat there for the whole ride with his mouth hanging open and his eyes goggled wide, staring blankly, not knowing what to say. A couple of times he opened his mouth and closed it, like a mackerel flopping on the dock. I believe he actually thought words were coming out. Molly sat there next to Warren, grinning like somebody had made her the queen of everything, and I don't think that had anything to do with the prime minister being in town.

"I wouldn't have missed this for the world," Molly told me.

As we drove along Main Street, the crowd all waved and cheered. Even those folks who had made a big deal out of bragging about how they hadn't even voted for this prime minister were there cheering along. This was a big day for Deeper Harbour—all of these tourists and the prime minister too—and everybody in town was determined to show their appreciation.

Personally, I didn't really see what the big deal was. I mean, the guy didn't look much like a prime minister ought to. He looked more like a middle-aged accountant or maybe a geography teacher. He had soft grey hair, faded into the colour of newsprint. He had heavy cheeks that sagged from his face like a pair of tired-out sails. Worse yet were his pointy nose and about three and a half chins that receded gradually into his flabby neck.

He did have a nice smile, although I noticed it mostly came out when a camera was pointed in his direction. It was like he had a secret mutant spider sense that some how homed in on the click of a camera shutter.

Mom gushed a bit and talked like a mayor for a while and then it was my turn. I had been sitting there thinking hard about what I would say to the prime minister of Canada, but the best I could up with was something lame.

"So what's Ottawa like?" I asked.

Like I said, lame.

"It's a wonderful city," the prime minister said, ignoring the fact that I had asked one of the lamest and most stupid questions in the universe. "I'm sure you will enjoy it."

I was beginning to think that might be true. I mean, maybe there was another world out there and maybe it would be kind of interesting to get to visit it.

"Ottawa always reminds me of a little town that grew up to be a city," the prime minister went on. "Everybody seems to know everybody else, just like here."

Mom nodded.

Warren made another fish mouth.

"This is really a beautiful little town," the prime minister told me. "You're really a lucky boy, growing up here."

And then he smiled. For just an instant it wasn't a have-I-told-you-I'm-the-prime-minister kind of smile, but an actual gee-it's-good-to-see-you kind of smile.

"Yeah," I said. "I guess I am kind of lucky."

We got out of the car and walked through the crowd to the wharf. The town had built a big platform close to Warren's boat shed. Over the door of the shed, Warren had hung a brand new sign that Granddad Angus had carved him:

"Boudreau's Boat Building—Home of Fine Dories Since 1832."

Warren hadn't been all that sure of the date, but Granddad Angus had assured him that eighteen-anything was historical enough for most people. As an afterthought, Warren had thumbtacked up a bristol board sign that read, "Ask Me About My Historical Stamps."

After he saw the second sign, the prime minister got a little excited because it turned out that he was a stamp collector as well. He asked Warren a few questions about his collection and Warren got to actually say a few words and a couple of actual sentences rather than just making fish-gawp sounds.

We all stepped up on the platform. It was covered with enough ribbons and bows for half-a-thousand birthday parties. It was kind of neat standing up there beside the prime minister of Canada and my mom and even boring old Warren and Molly, looking at the whole town looking up at me.

Everyone was talking about how grand it was that the prime minister of Canada had come to make a speech in our little town of

Deeper Harbour, but I had the feeling that they were more worked up about the chance of somebody famous spotting the sea monster.

Our sea monster.

A part of me felt pleased and proud that we had actually gone and done it. Granddad Angus and Warren and Dulsie and me, we had gone and built ourselves a legend. The whole country would be talking about Deeper Harbour.

This was our monster.

Deeper Harbour's monster.

I looked at the crowd. I could see Dad down there, standing at the edge of the crowd. I knew he was watching to make sure nobody got trampled.

I also knew he was watching for me.

I waved, thinking that he couldn't see me.

Except he waved back.

And then a hush fell over the crowd as if a giant wave of silence had swept over them and we finally saw the Deeper Harbour sea monster, slowly pedal-paddling its way into the mouth of the harbour.

I grinned so hard I thought my teeth might break.

Things couldn't get any better than they were.

And then things got worse.

Chapter 30

LONDON BRIDGE IS FALLING DOWN

"There he is," somebody shouted. Like a wave, everybody pushed closer to the edge of the wharf.

There were a lot of people cramming themselves onto that tired old wharf.

I could see my dad out there waving his arms, trying to hold them back.

The truth was, nobody had been sure they'd see Fogopogo today, foggy or not. He had only put in an appearance once or twice a week. A lot of people were worried about what the visitors might think if the monster didn't show up. I think that's why they had gone to so much effort to put on a show that would be worth it even if the Fogopogo hadn't appeared.

But here he was.

It was weird and exciting seeing Fogopogo out there.

I had never seen the monster from this angle before. I was used to seeing him from the inside.

It was a little like hearing a recording of my own voice and thinking, "Gosh, do I really sound like a squeaky, high-pitched, steamrollered mouse?"

That's sort of how I felt right now.

Now, standing beside my mom and the prime minister of Canada watching the sea monster that me and Warren and Dulsie and Granddad Angus had built, without the stink of the nine-hundred-year-old moose hide and the creaking of the pedal-paddles and the reek of the mopped paint, it looked a whole lot different than what I was used to.

"Now that's really cool," the prime minister said.

And then he whistled in genuine appreciation.

I almost broke out laughing.

How many people in the world can actually say that they've heard the prime minister of Canada say "cool" before?

I bet no one.

Nobody says "cool" these days but Dad and me, and even then Granddad Angus always laughed at us for it.

But that sorry old sea monster sure did look cool. In fact, it looked super-cool. Super-ultra-deep-fried-grilled-cheesy-cool to the maximum-squared-eternity-cool times cool.

It looked freaking near amazing.

Somehow Granddad Angus had created a cloud of smoke around it. It didn't look like woodsmoke to me, which was good, because starting a fire in a dory is a surefire way to sink yourself. It looked more like a weird kind of mist, like it was seeping out of Fogopogo's belly. And then all at once, Fogopogo's nostrils lit up like the trail of sparks from a skate sharpener. I heard people saying "ooh" and "ahh," like they were looking at a display of Canada Day fireworks going off.

"Well now," I heard the prime minister say to my mom, "that sure is something."

Warren kept gawking, his mouth hanging open. I was worried a fly was going to land in it. But he was grinning while he gawked. He was grinning like somebody had turned on a time machine and sent him back to when he was five years old and at his very first Santa Claus parade. And Molly was grinning right along with him.

Everything was super-duper-uber-cool.

People kept pushing and cramming excitedly onto the wharf.

SNAP!

Suddenly, a supporting timber broke loose and the wharf sort of tilted and leaned and then began to slide down towards the harbour.

I saw Dad waving his arms—half in panic, half in an attempt to keep order—as the crowd slowly slid towards him. Some people fell right in, while others managed to hang on by their fingernails. The whole wharf just sort of hung there for a minute, rocking in the tide, dangling like a broken trap door.

Everything was on a tilt and the old wood was slick with the salt spray. It didn't help that the morning mist had coated everything with a soft, wet, slickery dew.

A CBC cameraperson skidded and fell backwards with the weight of his camera and slid like an enormous curling stone, giving television viewers an amazing twenty-three second panoramic view of the Deeper Harbour sky before he hit the water, frantically working the buckles of his camera straps.

A hot dog cart rolled down into the harbour, wieners and buns flying in every direction. The seagulls were going to have themselves a fine old feast. The cart knocked at least a half a dozen tourists into the Atlantic.

People were yelling and screaming.

I wasn't sure if I should scream too or just break out laughing. It was scary and funny and goofy all at the same time. I stared in amazement as the dancing fishermen, oars sticking out in all directions, snowplowed another dozen or so festival-goers into the waiting harbour water.

Things got crowded and confusing.

I lost sight of Dad.

I heard Mom yelling Dad's name.

I didn't stop to think. My feet said run and I went with it. I wasn't certain if I was running towards Granddad Angus, towards my Dad, or towards whatever lay there in front of me.

I leaped off of the podium, nearly breaking my leg as I sprawled butt-first onto the concrete.

I'm not saying it was pretty.

I rolled three times and stood up.

Mom was still yelling Dad's name.

The last dragon dancer tipped off of the wharf and landed with a splash.

I couldn't see where Dad was from my angle.

I ran for the wharf, my legs pumping hard, and all the while Fogopogo moved slowly towards the shore.

Chapter 31

IN OVER MY HEAD, ONE MORE TIME

I didn't look back once.

There wasn't a moment to spare for any sort of second thought.

I reached the edge of the land, leaned forward, and dove.

For half a moment I was airborne. I caught a quick glimpse below me.

The water was chowdered thick with people. Some were swimming, some were dog-paddling, most were grimly treading water. And then, all at once, I was in the water, kicking with the tide, when a wave caught hold of me and pushed me under the dirty harbour water.

"DAD!" I called, throwing my voice out as if it was a stone, but the word was drowned out as the waves washed over my head.

I looked up and saw nothing but an army of kicking feet. Some were barefoot, some still wore shoes. I tried my best not to swallow. I could feel the salty seawater burning at my eyes. I could feel it trying to slide in under my eyelids and between my lips.

My feet kept kicking, but the water was heavy inside my shoes, dragging me down. I was sure I'd hit bottom, but I remembered just how deep Granddad Angus had told me Deeper Harbour really was.

Deeper by fathoms.

Deeper beyond dreaming.

I kicked off one shoe. I kept on paddling. I tried to kick off the other, but it just stayed stuck. I swallowed water. I tasted salt and spit it out, swallowing a bit more. I splashed my hands upwards, like I was trying to catch onto the rungs of an invisible ladder.

My fingers tangled in somebody's shoelace. They kicked at me blindly.

I slid back down. I felt the surface of the ocean slipping through my fingers as I started to sink.

I expected to see fish.

I expected to see stars.

I expected to see starfish.

All I could see was slow and cold and forever as I felt myself sinking down and I thought about how much I wanted to reach my dad.

Maybe Warren will save me like he did before.

Maybe Granddad Angus will save me.

Maybe Mom, or Molly, or the prime minister will save me.

And then all at once I pushed upwards and broke out of the water and drew in a deep breath.

I hadn't needn't anyone to save me but myself.

I looked around right after I had surfaced. Mom was there in the water beside Dad. The two of them were caught up in towing me in to safety. Mom didn't look a bit like the mayor. Her hair was flat with the weight of water and the makeup that she had spent so long putting on this morning was streaked like the end of a today tattoo.

This is all going to work out, I thought.

Mom and Dad would learn to love each other and they wouldn't get a divorce and we wouldn't have to move to Ottawa.

We were going to live happily ever after.

All of these thoughts flooded into my imagination while Fogopogo kept sailing straight towards the shoreline without me noticing a thing.

Chapter 32

TOSSED LIKE
SEA FOAM

The wharf was ruined.

The only way back to shore was up over the rough rocks near the old fish plant.

Mom and Dad and I dragged ourselves up onto the shore of Deeper Harbour, reeking of old fish and looking a little like members of an invading amphibious army who'd had the sea slime kicked out of them about two thousand leagues from the harbour.

I collapsed on the beach and looked around to see the rest of the wharf-wrecked survivors crawling up onto the rocks and coastal scree of the shoreline. Some of them managed a determined clamber while others were just tossed ashore by the waves like foam on the beach.

I'm not saying it was pretty.

Still, everybody seemed to be working together in that uncanny camaraderie that only a disaster can bring about. Those who had escaped the unexpected dunking threw ropes and lifesavers and tugged and towed people who weren't so lucky onto dry land. A few brave souls even dove in and dog-paddled nearly drowned tourists and townsfolk to safety.

That's just how a town works, I guess.

"The monster's getting closer!" somebody shouted.

Everyone's attention turned back to Fogopogo.

I looked up and could see that the monster was not more than a hundred feet from the shore—and getting closer.

Ha!

I guessed that Granddad Angus was coming closer to help the people who were still in the water. I had to grin at the thought of their faces as a full-grown sea monster pulled up to rescue them. Still, even though I knew it was the right thing to do, I was a little angry that Granddad Angus was spoiling our trick.

And then, all at once, the monster stopped moving forward and started to drift with the tidal current. I could tell that Granddad Angus had stopped pedalling and was just letting the dory drift. I guessed that he was just catching his breath for a while.

Only Fogopogo kept on drifting.

What was Granddad Angus up to? He had surprised me with the smoke and the fire-breathing. Maybe he had some other trick up his sleeve. Or hidden in one of his many vest pockets.

But nothing was happening. Fogopogo just sat there, rocking gently in the waves, caught up against a sea boulder.

I began to worry.

Something was wrong.

Something was really wrong.

"It's coming this way," somebody shouted.

"It's angry," somebody else said.

"It's going to eat us all!" somebody else screamed.

And then somebody shouted "Dad!"

I sat there on the beach, half-drowned, staring in utter

amazement as Dad half-ran and half-shambled down towards the water. He waded out until it was deep enough to swim. I felt Mom catching onto my shoulder. I think Dulsie had a hold on my other shoulder, but I could not be stopped.

I twisted away from Mom.

I heard something got crack in my shoulder. Maybe I had pulled my arm off but I didn't care.

I fell down and stood up and kicked off like I was a human speed demon. I ran out into the waiting water to follow my father back into the sea.

Things got deeper fast.

Chapter 33

THE LAST KNOCK-
KNOCK JOKE

It wasn't nearly as deep as I had dreamed it to be.

Dad and I waded out to the dory and dragged Fogopogo to shore. Other people came out and helped us drag. I saw Warren and Dulsie and even the prime minister.

I pushed past them all, and wormed my way under to look beneath the nine-hundred-year-old moose hide. It was a misty blur inside the monster. Granddad Angus had laid a few pans of dry ice on the bottom of the dory, which had made the mist that we had all seen. The fiery nostrils were nothing more than two sets of three lit sparklers twist-tied together.

It was a cold, smoky mess in there.

Granddad Angus was leaning against the portside pedal.

His face was as pale as fresh fallen snow and his eyes were glazed in a deep, faraway kind of stare.

"Get him up out of there," I heard my dad saying, somewhere close behind my right ear. "It's his heart."

Granddad Angus reached out and caught me with one hand on my shoulder blade.

"Did it fool them all?" he asked.

I tried to say something, but my mouth wouldn't work.

"It fooled everybody, Dad," I heard my father say. "You sure as shooting fooled everybody."

Granddad Angus grinned and for just a moment I thought he was going to stand up and walk.

"When did you figure out it was me?" he asked.

"Who else in Deeper Harbour was fool enough to build themselves a sea monster?" Dad asked.

Granddad Angus tried to laugh, only he leaned back as if the funny hurt.

"It was something, wasn't it?"

"It sure was, Dad."

"I'll take this with me," he said.

And then he leaned back as if everything had run out of his body all at once.

"Don't you dare let go," my dad said. "Don't you dare let go."

Granddad Angus nodded weakly.

"Don't you let go either," he said.

"You taught me everything that I know," Dad said.

"I learned as much from raising you as I could ever have hoped to learn," Granddad Angus said. "You taught me more than you'll ever know."

He grinned a shadowy, tattered ghost of a grin and I could see my dad's grin hiding behind Granddad Angus's grin and behind that the grin I saw in the mirror every morning.

"I'm done now."

And then he was gone.

"Well, that was truly something."

I looked.

The prime minister of Canada was standing there beside me, his trousers bagged in seawater, staring at my dead Granddad Angus and my dad who was crying as hard as I had ever seen him cry. All the while he stood there, shaking his head and sort of gently half-grinning, not knowing whether to laugh or cry.

Granddad Angus was gone.

Dad was drowning in tears.

Dulsie and Warren were holding onto each other and Molly was holding on as tight as she could to the two of them. Everybody else who crowded around was still trying to decide what exactly had just happened in this harbour.

I looked up and saw Mom standing there on the beach alone.

I waded ashore and walked towards her, my steps heavy, as if I were wading into a deep, cold stream.

PART V

VIKING FAREWELL

Chapter 34

LEGAL IS AS LEGAL DOES

We buried Granddad Angus in a field just beyond the fence of his old house, underneath one of the trees. A tattered old birch tree, with the bark peeling off like it was waiting for somebody to write something on it.

Only I couldn't think of any words that would fit.

Mom sang "Amazing Grace." Dad just hummed along and tapped his foot several beats out of time. Warren sang something soft and Gaelic in a surprisingly fine tenor. I didn't know what the words of the song meant and I didn't know how to ask him at such a time, but a part of me felt that Granddad Angus would have understood and would have appreciated the deep Celtic mystery of it all.

"This isn't legal, is it?" I asked. "Burying somebody outside of a graveyard?"

"I'm the police chief and your mother's the mayor," Dad said. "That's as legal as it needs to get, here in Deeper Harbour."

I cried.

Mom cried.

Dad cried.

Dulsie cried.

Warren dragged a handkerchief out of his pocket and fog-horned his nose a little.

All of us stood there around my grandfather's grave, letting our tears splash in the dirt together. Us crying together wasn't going to change anything, but it felt good and bad and sad all at the very same time.

Then Mom took Dad's hand and squeezed it a little.

Dad smiled.

I thought again that everything was going to be okay.

And then Mom let go in a movement that wasn't really sudden.

I had seen it coming all along.

I could hear the waves lapping at the beach, like a kid eating a forever ice cream cone on a hot summer day.

The three of us drifted gently apart.

Chapter 35

UNDER THE COVER
OF MOOSE HIDE

Three days later Dad lugged an old trolling motor out of the
garage.

"It's time," he said.

And so it was.

We walked down to the harbour where the dory monster still
stood, moored next to Warren's boat shed. People had already begun to tear down and cart away the ruins of the wharf. They would
rebuild and restore it and Deeper Harbour would go on.

Most of the town stood around, quietly watching and waiting
for what they knew was to come. Nora deep-fried some sandwiches, but no one seemed the least bit hungry. A lot of them were
firmly convinced that Granddad Angus had built that sea monster
dory as part of the Fogopogo Festival celebration.

People are funny that way. It was like they had come to believe
so deeply in Fogopogo that they didn't want to let go of the dream.
Of course it might have been that they were thinking with their
wallets and trying to make sure that the tourists kept on coming,
but a part of me believes that there was a lot more to it than that.

Which makes me glad.

"Wasn't he worried that Fogopogo would get after him?" some wanted to know.

"It looks just like the real thing," others said.

"How do you think he ran it all by himself?" somebody asked me.

I just shook my head.

I think more than a few of them suspected that Granddad Angus had some extra help and that our dory monster was actually what had caused all the trouble in the first place—but if they did, they were keeping their mouths tightly shut.

The twelve fishermen had dried out their dragon and danced up a gumbooted storm in tribute to Granddad Angus.

"I bet you he would have liked to have seen this," I said.

"I bet you he's watching us right now," Dulsie said.

Warren had brewed up some tea and Dad and I stood and sipped and blew. Dad was wearing Granddad Angus's magic fishing vest of many pockets. I hadn't seen Dad take it, but I guessed it was only right.

"I want to keep this," Dad said.

I didn't argue.

After the tea, Dad strapped the trolling motor to the dory monster. I had one last look inside the moose hide. I wanted to see it one more time. I wanted to take it all in and store it in a deep part of my memory. I wanted to memorize every joint and nail and sliver.

Which was when I saw what Granddad Angus had been working on the night before the last ride of the dory monster. I felt it first, touching with my fingertips something gouged in the oak of the dory's walls. A word, carefully carved.

I pulled the edge of the moose hide away and read the word that Granddad Angus had carved there.

A single name.

Marjorie.

A part of me wondered just why he'd carved it there.

Had he known he was going to die like he did?

Or maybe he just that proud of all that he and Dulsie and Warren and I had done this summer.

I didn't know the answer.

I didn't know if I ever would.

So I just let the moose hide fall back to cover that name.

Some stories are told better without words.

Some stories are meant to be whispered in the dark.

"It's time," Dad said again.

Just before I stepped back I grabbed hold of the amethyst eyes and pulled them off the dory monster, from where Granddad Angus had stuck them.

"I want to keep these," I said. "One for me and one for Warren."

Dad just nodded.

Then he poured a can of kerosene into the belly of the sea monster dory and lit the lantern and set it on my purple glitter banana seat.

He turned on the engine and the monster chugged into the harbour.

Chumma-chumma-chumma.

Warren stepped out of his shed, dressed in a kilt and full Highland regalia, carrying a set of bagpipes.

I've said it before and I'll say it again.

People can surprise you.

Mom and Molly and Dulsie stood just a little behind Warren.

Dulsie had a surprise for me as well. She wasn't wearing one bit of a today tattoo. For the first time in as long as I could remember, Dulsie Jane Boudreau looked just like herself.

Warren played a pibroch as the dory monster chumma-chumma-chummed out into the harbour. About halfway out the motion of the waves must have tipped the lantern over. I saw a brief flash of light, like a shooting star falling out of the sky.

The sea monster dory burned, raising a large cloud of smoke that I was certain would be seen far out at sea.

I reached into my pockets and squeezed the amethyst eyes that I had taken from Fogopogo.

There are things you hang on to and things you have to learn to let go.

"Ottawa will be a big change," Dad said. "You'll be in deep water for sure."

I thought about that.

"I know how to swim," I said. "You and Granddad Angus taught me how."

Dad looked at me.

"Ottawa won't be so bad," I said.

And it isn't.

Chapter 36

LEARNING TO LET GO

The amethyst eye of the sea monster sits on my bedside table, winking at me from the darkness. I hung Granddad Angus's old saw over my bed with baling wire and screws. It's a good thing that there aren't any earthquakes here in Ottawa because if that old saw ever fell off of the wall it just might cut me in half.

Dad phones me at least once a week. He and Warren have gone into business together. They've made a museum out of the old boat shed. They've got pictures of the dory monster and a picture of Granddad Angus. Warren sells and trades his postage stamps and Dad gets to talk about history and they've moved Molly's library into the shed, too. They're even talking about building a new library in a few years, but I think Molly likes it where she is just fine.

Tourists are still coming. There is a new bus line running from Halifax to Deeper Harbour. Business is booming and the town is doing fine.

Dulsie has decided that when she finishes high school, she'll go to art college. She writes me letters at least once a week, with sketches and cartoons on every page. I really think that she ought to become a cartoonist, but she has it in her mind that one day she'll own and run her own tattoo shop—and maybe she will.

Three months after Granddad Angus's Viking funeral, David Suzuki finally showed up with a film crew to shoot a *Nature of Things* episode on cryptids and urban and rural mythology. Dad let him spend the night in my jail cell and Warren chucked an honorary caber, which flattened the camera van and nearly murdered David Suzuki.

David Suzuki wasn't bothered by the attempted caber-assassination, though. He was more excited about the new species of tree he discovered growing in Molly's backyard. A long and gangly Nova Scotia Jack pine, with a scent that haunted in your nostrils like a mixture of pine cones and freshly baked pumpkin pie.

I don't know if any coyotes howl under it every night but they ought to.

Some nights, I take the big old saw down and make it into that funny-looking s-curve and play it a little. It doesn't sound nearly as pretty as it did when Granddad Angus played it, but I'm working on it.

Sometimes I cry a little when I'm playing. Not big boo-hoo kind of sobbing, just slow tears sneaking down my cheek. I think about my Granddad Angus—the most important person in my whole short life. When the tear reaches the crease of my lip, I catch the teardrop with my tongue, and think of sea water.

Some nights I just lie here in my bed and breathe in and breathe out—long, slow, deep breaths—and I imagine that my breath is touching the very same air that my Dad is breathing a thousand miles away and in the breathing I can hear the sound of the waves washing in on Deeper Harbour.

I breathe deep.

My eyes are clear.

A brand new morning is moments away.

It is no mechanic's file through a jailhouse window, but for right here and right now it is all the alarm clock I need.

ACKNOWLEDGMENTS

When I was seventeen years old I came from Northern Ontario to visit Nova Scotia and to meet my mother—whom I barely knew. It was to be nothing more than a very short visit. This short visit has lasted over thirty-five years. So I'd like to thank the province of Nova Scotia and all the wonderful people I have met here for taking me into their hearts and making me feel completely at home.

I would also like to acknowledge my Aunt Marjorie—a lovely lady who passed away in early September 2010. I'm sorry I didn't get there soon enough to say goodbye.

A big tip of my hat must also go to the great folks at Nimbus and all the help they gave me getting this book into print. Thanks to Penelope, Patrick, Terrilee, and all the rest of you hardworking people.

Thanks to Mom for believing in my writing.

Thanks to my lovely wife, Belinda, for believing in me—as always you remain my one true love. You have taught me that life and love have a deeper meaning.

Other books by Steve Vernon:

Haunted Harbours
Wicked Woods
Halifax Haunts

Children's picture books

Maritime Monsters